CAPTAIN'S DAY

by

Terry Ravenscroft

**Grosvenor House
Publishing Limited**

This book is published by
Grosvenor House Publishing Ltd
28-30 High Street, Guildford, Surrey, GU1 3HY.
www.grosvenorhousepublishing.co.uk

A CIP record for this book
is available from the British Library

ISBN 978-1-907211-35-5

Cover artwork by Tony Colligan   www.tctoons.com

CAPTAIN'S DAY

Terry Ravenscroft

....Until six months ago Phyllis Hill had been Philip Hill, at which point in his life he had undertaken a sex-change operation. (Armitage, with a possible penis transplant in mind, had enquired as to the size of the unwanted genitalia, but Philip had told him that Phyllis would be holding on to it, figuratively speaking, for sentimental reasons.)

Up until the time of the operation Philip had been a transvestite and when playing golf had dressed as do most lady golfers, in pastel shades and tweedy things, and well-cut trousers, rather than a skirt. Thus attired he could quite easily have been taken for one of the lady members at Sunnymere, not because he looked particularly feminine but because quite a few of the more heftily built lady members could easily be taken for transvestites....

CAPTAIN'S DAY

Terry Ravenscroft was born in the town of New Mills in the Peak District of Derbyshire. His mother had a particularly long and difficult delivery, largely because she'd forgotten to take off her tights. Terry remained naked for the first four years of his life as his parents were so poor they couldn't afford to buy him clothes; then the local vicar felt sorry for him and bought him a hat so he could look out of the window. His parents decided to share equally the responsibility of bringing up their son; however he proved to be a difficult baby, often throwing tantrums and crying for long spells, especially when it was his father's turn to breast feed him. But he eventually grew out of it, prospered, and at the age of five started his formal education. He was a bright child at school as his mother had painted his head with luminous paint so she could pick him out easily when she came to collect him. Despite this inauspicious beginning to his life, or perhaps because of it, he grew up to be a comedy scriptwriter for such stars as Les Dawson, The Two Ronnies and Morecambe and Wise. He now writes humorous books, such as the one you are at this moment considering buying. Don't do it, you will only encourage him.

Also by Terry Ravenscroft

Football Crazy
Air Mail
Dear Customer Services

The above titles are available from bookshops and Amazon, price £6.99 each, or I can supply signed copies direct at no extra cost, post free. Simply visit my website or email me with your requirements.

Terry Ravenscroft

terryrazz@gmail.com   www.topcomedy.co.uk

PREFACE

Today, Saturday the 25th of July 2009, is Captain's Day at Sunnymere Golf Club. In addition to Mr Captain, who quite naturally we will be seeing a great deal of, and his good lady wife Millicent, we will be meeting many other people who have been brought together on this, the most important day in a golf club's calendar. Amongst them will be Robin Garland, the vice-captain of the club, known to one and all as Mr Vice, who doesn't have too good a day of it; and Andrew Arbuthnott, the club treasurer, who has a much better day of it, choosing the occasion to play the best golf of his life. We will be meeting George Fidler, a man who always plays Top Flight four golf balls, until today that is, and Richard Irwin, a man who firmly believes that ladies should be allowed on the golf course each and every day between one-o-clock and six-o-clock....a.m. We will spend time with long but wayward hitter Dogleg Davies; Sylvester Cuddington, a man who is the proud owner of a newly-modelled golf swing; club throwers supreme Dave Tollemache and Graham Burton; the orally challenged Rhys Jones-Jones; and Trevor Armitage, a man whose mind is not always one hundred per cent on his golf. We will meet The Red Arrows; club professional Dave Tobin and his new assistant, Darren; the cheating Adams brothers; several of the lady members; the weird and wonderful Phyllis Hill and the even more weird and wonderful Dance DJ Daddy Rhythm. Finally we will be meeting a few people one wouldn't ordinarily expect to find on a golf course; police officers Fearon and James; firemen Jeffers and Blakey; helicopter pilot Green and film cameraman Morton; two young lovers; and members of the press and local radio. So welcome one and all to Captain's Day. Have a good round.

In an ideal world the person chosen to be the captain of a golf club, all things being equal, would be the most suitable candidate available. However it is not an ideal world and things are very rarely equal; a fair number of the club's members will not have the time to devote to a position which has so many demands placed upon it, whilst others, even if they have the time, do not have the inclination. On these occasions it is possible for a less than ideal person to be chosen for the job. At Sunnymere Golf Club such a year was 2009.

Mr Captain 2009 vintage, one Henry Fridlington, was a man who, not to put too fine a point on it, was full of his own importance. It was difficult to see why, for if he had achieved little eminence in his career as a cost and works accountant he had achieved even less in his chosen sport of golf, never aspiring to anything better than a very dodgy 19 handicap, which by the time of his captaincy was back up to 23 and counting. Henry applied himself to cost and works accounting in the wholly stolid, methodical manner he felt the vocation demanded, whereas he played golf with the optimistic verve of a Severiano Ballesteros, but unfortunately with none of that artist's great skill. It is a sad fact that had he applied himself to golf the way he applied himself to accountancy and applied himself to accountancy the way he did to golf he would have made a far better job of them both. But he didn't, and so, although a man full of his own importance, he had nothing of which to feel full of importance about. Nevertheless he was full of it; and particularly so today, Saturday the twenty fifth of July 2009. Because today was Captain's Day. His day.

It would be impossible to overstress the significance of the occasion to Henry. Nothing of such momentous importance had happened to an individual since time began. Possibly Nelson's famous victory at Trafalgar or

1

Winston Churchill's finest hour might run it a distant second, but no more than that. And in the field of sport Jonny Wilkinson's part in bringing the Rugby Union World Cup to England and Freddie Flintoff's heroics in recapturing the Ashes didn't come anywhere near to it in magnitude.

Now, as he dressed for the occasion, Mr Captain went over in his mind for about the one hundredth time the Captain's Day's arrangements that had been made. Meticulous planning by he and his wife Millicent, a past captain of the ladies section herself, would ensure that the day would go without a hitch. Everything had been put in place to make it a perfect day. Nothing had been left to chance. The Captain's Day dinner dance that evening would be a huge success, the best ever. The dinner itself would be excellent. The main course, poached cod and boiled potatoes, would go down very well, literally, although it might not go down very well metaphorically with those diners who had complained there wasn't an alternative to poached cod and boiled potatoes; and it would not go down at all, neither literally nor metaphorically, with the twenty two members of the club who had refused to attend the event when they found out what they were expected to eat that evening.

The reason Mr Captain had chosen poached cod and boiled potatoes was not because he was particularly fond of the dish but because he had recently been troubled with a duodenal ulcer, and to help keep it under control his doctor had put him on a fat and fried food-free diet. Mr Captain could of course have gone for a menu of roast duck, roast potatoes and green peas, with maybe a roast beef alternative, and certainly a vegetarian option, as suggested by the club secretary, and just had poached cod and boiled potatoes himself, but the problem with that arrangement was that he was quite partial to roast duck, roast potatoes and green peas and couldn't bear the thought of everyone else eating and enjoying it whilst he himself was forced to eat poached cod and boiled potatoes. So poached cod and boiled potatoes was what everyone would be dining on, and people could like it or lump it, and as far as the vegetarians were concerned he simply dismissed their dietary requirements as 'faddy'.

The dance part of the dinner dance would be sure to go with a swing, not least because this year the music would be provided not by a noisy disco, as had become the norm over the last few years, but by a four-piece band, led by the ex-lead trumpeter of Jimmy Shand and his Band, no less.

The number of tickets sold for the event was a bit down on previous years, partly due to the twenty two members who had refused point blank to be tempted by the delights of poached cod and boiled potatoes, but mainly because unfortunately the event clashed with Ant and Dec's Disabled Under-Fives Commonwealth Song Contest, or some such, on television - or so quite a few members who usually attended the Captain's Day dinner dance had claimed. In fact so many members had decided to give the event a miss it had led Mr Captain into suspecting that the snub must be rooted in some sort of conspiracy. Well Mr Captain could conspire too; he knew who wasn't coming who normally attended the event, and in future would be keeping a special watch on them for any contravention of the golf club rules, and in particular the bad language regulations.

The competitions within the Captain's Prize competition had been organised; the Nearest the Pin competition, the Golden Ferret competition, and the Longest Drive competition. But not the Shortest Drive competition, an event that had been introduced by last year's Mr Captain as a bit of a laugh, but which had been dropped by this year's Mr Captain as he couldn't see anything to laugh about in the holding of such a competition; not, as some had claimed, because it was he himself who had hit the shortest drive and had in consequence been awarded the inaugural Duffer's Cup, which he had refused to accept, but because he considered it to be far too frivolous a diversion to be included in such a momentous occasion as Captain's Day.

The previous day the beer tent had been erected on the stretch of spare land between the first tee and the ninth green. Having the beer tent would cost him a pretty penny, even allowing for the fact that he would be monitoring consumption to ensure it was limited to strictly one drink per player, but it would be more than well worth it.

And the weather would be ideal. The sun was already warm even at this early hour; the sky was blue with not a cloud in sight, a perfect English summer's day. Even the best planned Captain's Day would be a slight disappointment if the weather turned out to be bad, so he hadn't taken any chances and the previous evening had prayed to God for nice weather. And God had come up trumps. Mr Captain had known He would, even though the last time he'd called upon the Almighty for assistance his chrysanthemums had taken only second place at the annual flower show instead of the first place he had prayed for, the top prize having been taken, unaccountably to Mr Captain, by a man on the sex-offenders register.

Mr Captain now flicked an imaginary speck of dust from the lapel of his blazer and turned from the full length bedroom mirror to his wife. "How do I look, Millicent?"

The question was superfluous for he had no real need to ask. He knew how he looked. The mirror had told him. Immaculate, from top to toe. The burgundy captain's blazer with the gold club badge emblazoned on the breast pocket, just enough spotless white handkerchief protruding from the pocket, the starched white shirt, the burgundy and yellow striped Sunnymere club tie, the grey plus four trousers, the rather racy-looking flat cap and matching socks in the tartan of the Campbell clan (Mr Captain had no connection with the Campbells, apart from a fondness for their condensed cream of chicken soup, but the colours and design of the tartan appealed to him), the whole ensemble was just so.

"You look very smart, darling," said Millicent. "I am very proud of you."

And so you might well be, thought Mr Captain, and so you might well be. After all it isn't every member of a golf club who aspires to its captaincy. One has to be made of the right stuff. He was made of the right stuff, he was sure. Hadn't he proved as much with the introduction and implementation of his Captain's Project?

It was the tradition at Sunnymere Golf Club that during his year of office the incumbent captain implemented a project of his choice, known as the Captain's Project, which would be of lasting benefit to the club. The captain could choose anything he liked within reason. Two years ago the then Mr Captain, by raising the necessary finance through donations, raffles, pro-ams, sponsored golfathons, car boot sales and other fund-raising activities, and enlisting voluntary labour from amongst the membership, had planted the 2000 new trees that now bordered the third, fifth, eighth and seventeenth fairways, and which in years to come would both enhance the beauty of the course whilst making it slightly more difficult to negotiate.

Last year's Mr Captain had vowed to double the membership of the junior section and to further encourage junior golf in any way possible, with particular regard to coaching the youngsters in the etiquette and skills of the game. Not only did he more than double the membership but he took the juniors to a runner's up spot in the County Championships, their highest placed finish in the club's history.

Mr Captain knew that such projects were beyond his scope, even if it would benefit the course to have a further 2000 trees planted or to double the junior membership yet again. Truth to be told it was less trees and fewer junior members cluttering up the course that he was in favour of, not more; he had enough trouble with the former as things already stood and more than enough dislike of the latter. Anyway his Captain's Project would be far more beneficial to the club than a few straggly trees and more loud-mouthed spotty youths.

Initially it had been his intention to give lady golfers unlimited access to the course at all times. Such a revolutionary act would not only have put him in the good books of the lady members for ever more, and especially in those of his wife, but it would also have got right up the

5

noses of the male members, the vast majority of whom he didn't get on with.

The complete banning of mobile phones on the golf course had been another strong possibility (at the moment they could be carried provided they were switched off). If Mr Captain had had his way he would have banned mobile phones not only from the golf course but from the face of the earth. He had never been able to find anything in favour of them and had no trouble finding several things against them, the main one being that it was a mobile phone which had caused him to have an air shot when it had rung just as he had started his downswing on his approach shot to the tenth in the Sunnymere Silver Salver last year. Not only had it cost him a penalty shot but probably the competition as well, as following the incident his game had gone completely to pieces, and far from a victory had resulted in him ripping up his card for the third week running.

A third possibility, and the hot favourite for a long time, was to ban Sunday competitions. A dedicated churchgoer, Mr Captain would have liked to have banned all Sunday play, and would have done so had he not felt that such an action would not be tolerated by the membership, despite it being a Captain's Project.

In the normal course of events all the club competitions, both monthly medals and majors, were played on Saturdays and Sundays, split approximately fifty-fifty between the two. It had been Mr Captain's intention to move all the Sunday competitions to Saturdays, thus leaving people free to attend church.

He had no axe to grind with people who played golf on Sunday, indeed he often played on Sundays himself, but when he did he always ensured that he attended morning service when he played in the afternoons and evening service when he played in the mornings.

When he had made known his intentions it was pointed out to him, again by the ever vigilant club secretary, that the majority of the membership would not attend church even if they had all day Sunday free in which to do so plus the rest of the week as well, and that for many of them it would take the introduction of pole dancers in the aisle and a free bar and buffet in the vestry in order for them to attend, but in answer to this Mr Captain had replied that if people chose to be heathens then that was their lookout.

In the end however, and as appealing as these three candidates for his Captain's Project were, he came up with an even more worthy idea. To rid the club once and for all of bad language. In particular the 'F' word and the 'C' word. But the 'T' word also, along with the 'S 'word and all the 'B' words. When he had made his plans known, immediately upon taking office, the General Committee, whilst agreeing it would be a very good thing, had expressed grave doubts about its worthiness as a Captain's Project. Not a few of the members had said it was unreasonable, a few more thought it unworkable.

Mr Captain however would have none of their objections and had insisted that to make the fairways and greens 'F' and 'C' word free would benefit the entire membership of the club and 'not just people who liked trees and juniors'. There was no further discussion. No argument. Nor could there be. The Captain could choose as his project anything within reason which he saw fit, and he saw his Captain's Project as being well within reason and very fit indeed. A notice had been put up on the club notice board the following day.

BAD LANGUAGE

It has been brought to the notice of the General Committee that certain members of the club are using bad language on the golf course. This is both unnecessary and undesirable. Use of the F-word and the C-word is particularly abhorrent. In an effort to stamp this out once and for all, and with immediate effect, any member found to be using the F-word or the C-word or any other swear word will be required to appear before the General Committee with a view to immediate expulsion from the club.

Mr Captain

The first two golfers to read the notice were Greg Coleman and Richard Irwin.

"Fuck me!" said Coleman.

"The cunt!" said Irwin.

Fortunately Mr Captain had not been in earshot when the aggrieved pair had uttered the newly-banned expletives. However he was well within earshot on the occasion that eighteen handicapper Bradley Tomkinson leapt in the air in delight and yelled, "A fucking birdie, it's a fucking birdie!" on chipping in from the edge at the second. For this the unfortunate Tomkinson had been hauled before the committee and handed a final warning. Since then more than a dozen such final warnings had been issued. One poor golfer, already on a final warning, and who only erred the second time because he said 'Fuck!' when he dropped his sand wedge on the ingrowing toenail of his big toe, had been expelled.

Bad language on the golf course had plummeted. It still occurred of course, but those who used it now did so with discretion and not a little guile. For example when putting his name down for a club competition a golfer prone to using the odd swear word would ensure that he chose a starting time well away from that chosen by Mr Captain, thus giving himself the best possible chance of not being overheard if and when an errant swear word should accidentally pop out, which it is almost bound to, golf being golf.

After a final glance in the mirror Mr Captain breathed a contented sigh, pecked his wife on the cheek goodbye and left for the golf club to enjoy to the full his Captain's Day.

D Bagley (8)
G Chapman (9)
A Arbuthnott (11)

Shortly before 8.30 Mr Captain took up position beside the first tee. From there he would greet and see safely on their way each group of three golfers at the commencement of their round. Once the first threesome had reached the ninth green his intention was to operate between the first tee and the beer tent, still attending to his welcoming duties at the first tee whilst making time to enquire of each threesome what was their pleasure when they arrived at the beer tent after completing the ninth hole, and ensuring that their pleasure stopped at one drink.

The first threesome of the day, consisting of regular playing partners Des Bagley, Gerry Chapman and Andrew Arbuthnott, was now making its way leisurely to the first tee. All three golfers were looking forward to their round of golf, but especially so Arbuthnott, who felt in his water that this could well be the day he returned a winning card, and now said as much to the others.

"Your optimism knows no bounds, Andrew," observed Bagley, on hearing Arbuthnott's hopeful prognostication.

"No I can really sense it, Baggers. It was there the moment I woke up this morning, a sort of gut feeling, and it's been there ever since."

"Probably indigestion," said Chapman. "I think I've got some Alka-Seltzer tablets in my bag if you'd like a couple."

Arbuthnott shook his head. "Not indigestion Gerry. Just the deep conviction that I'm going to pull it off today."

"Arby you haven't won a competition in years, and even then it wasn't one of any account, why should today be any different?" reasoned Chapman, forever the pragmatist.

"No I always play well on Captain's Day," Arbuthnott insisted. "I was well in the running last year until I had that disaster at the sixteenth. The big occasion seems to bring out the best in me. And I'm really up for it this year; get the name of Andrew Arbuthnott up in gold at last."

Arbuthnott wanted to see his name on one of the roll of honour boards displayed in the clubhouse in tribute to the winners of major competitions almost as much as Henry Fridlington wanted his Captain's Day to be a huge success. His father had won the President's Putter competition and his father before him had triumphed in the Anderson Bowl and Arbuthnott felt he was letting the family name down by not being the third generation of the Arbuthnott dynasty to be so honoured.

"The only way you're ever going to get your name up in gold Arby is if you buy a shop and get a sign writer to write it over the top," said Chapman, with an air of cruel certainty that now caused doubt to enter Arbuthnott's mind for the first time that day.

"You'll see, Gerry, you'll see," said Arbuthnott, turning away and cutting short the conversation lest Chapman should say anything else that might sow a seed of doubt in his mind.

Although Mr Captain was undoubtedly the most unpopular captain there had ever been in the history of Sunnymere Golf Club the entire membership of the club treated him with due deference. The only person who had not shown the captain this respect, a member not only new to the club but also new to the game of golf, and who obviously wasn't aware of golf club protocol, had very quickly been informed that it is the position of Mr Captain that commands the respect of the membership and not the person holding that position, and from then on had treated Mr Captain with the same respect accorded him by all the other members. Thus it was that on arriving at the first tee Arbuthnott, Chapman and Bagley all greeted the captain with a dutiful chorus of "Good morning, Mr Captain." Arbuthnott felt so chipper about his chances that he followed up the salutation with a pleasantry he wouldn't normally have wasted on the present Mr Captain. "You're looking very smart."

"One has to set standards, Andrew," said Mr Captain, then, with no little pride, disclosed the secret he had been keeping on the back burner up until now. "Incidentally, I'm having the day filmed, so be sure to keep a sharp lookout for the cameras."

Arbuthnott was impressed. "Filmed?"

"It is a proud day in my life, Andrew. A very proud day. To be Mr Captain on Captain's Day is something that only happens to a man maybe once in his lifetime, consequently I decided to have the occasion recorded on video for posterity."

"What an excellent idea."

"I thought so," said Mr Captain, and went on, "Now be sure not to forget the Nearest the Pin competition on the thirteenth. Three of the ladies have kindly agreed to do the measuring this year."

Bagley expressed surprise on hearing this. Traditionally boys from the junior section had always been entrusted with this task on Captain's Day. "The ladies, Mr Captain?" he said, raising an eyebrow.

"Yes, nice to get the ladies involved, isn't it."

"I mean the juniors usually do it."

"I decided to ring the changes; and it is my wish that the ladies do the honours this time round."

"Wonderful," said Chapman.

"Isn't it," said Mr Captain, fully aware that Chapman was being facetious but not caring a fig about it one way or the other. If bigots like Gerry Chapman didn't like it then it was just too bad. He checked his watch. "Eight thirty precisely gentlemen, best be getting your round underway, you don't want to be holding up the rest of the field."

Bagley tipped his cap politely and the three golfers stepped onto the first tee.

The first at Sunnymere, as is the case with the opening holes on many golf courses, is a relatively easy par four. The reason for most opening holes being fairly straightforward is that there is less chance of the golfer, not yet fully into the swing of things, making a pig's ear of the job and ruining his round before he has hardly begun it, which in all probability is what might very well happen if the opening hole presented any sort of challenge. Quite simply an easy opening hole gives the golfer the opportunity to 'play himself in', and although most golfers, having played themselves in on the first hole, somehow contrive to play themselves out and ruin their card on the second hole, or one of the subsequent holes, an easy opening hole is still regarded as a good thing.

"Your honour I believe, Baggers," said Arbuthnott, in recognition of the fact that Bagley had the lowest handicap of the threesome and was thus entitled to tee off first.

Bagley strode confidently onto the tee and drove off, hitting his usual high fade of two hundred and twenty yards or so.

"Shot," said Mr Captain generously.

"I ought to be," said Bagley, forlornly. "Twenty years I've been playing this game and I still can't hit the ball much over two hundred yards."

"You've always had an excellent short game though Des," said Arbuthnott, offering encouragement to his playing partner whilst at the same time taking out a little insurance against Bagley moaning all the time if things weren't quite going his way, as he was wont to do, and possibly spoiling his own chances by putting him off his game.

Next to tee off was Chapman, who hit a poor shot off the toe of his driver. He followed the flight of the ball as it bounced once on the fairway before scuttling into the right-hand rough, then said, in honest judgement of his lamentable attempt at a drive, "Crap. Absolute crap."

There had been a long and intense debate in General Committee as to whether the word 'crap' was or was not a swear word. Mr Captain had maintained it was. However the majority of the committee had argued otherwise. In the end there had been a trade-off, Mr Captain allowing 'crap' on the understanding that 'twat' was added to the list of swear words. (It had been proposed that twat be an allowed word, several members of the committee claiming it meant the same as 'twit'. Mr Captain however argued differently. His Shorter Oxford had confirmed to him that a twit was someone who was a fool whereas a twat was someone who is considered to be worthless, unpleasant and despicable, and, having recently been called a twat by the window cleaner, who he had refused to pay because he hadn't got right into the corners of one of the bedroom windows with his wash leather, was well aware that the reason he had been called a twat was not because he had behaved like a twit.)

Last to drive was Arbuthnott, who hit an absolute boomer, all of two hundred and forty yards, straight down the middle. Mr Captain clapped his hands together in applause. "Oh good shot, Andrew. Excellent drive."

"Thank you Mr Captain," smiled Arbuthnott, then with his smile now taking on the hint of a smirk he turned to Chapman and said, "I told you it was going to be my day, didn't I."

—※—

Club professional Dave Tobin had just sold the latest fad in drivers to the first customer who had entered his shop that morning. That the new club would be of no use whatsoever to its proud new owner and that he would have been far better off dispensing altogether with the services of a driver and using a three iron to drive with, Tobin did not enlighten him. Nor would he ever. The professional had always held the opinion that the customer, whilst not necessarily always being right, was always one hundred per cent right when they were intent on buying the very latest in golf equipment. Tobin was also very well aware that even if he had tried to talk the customer out of the new driver it would have been a waste of breath, so why bother? Apart from that he wasn't in the golf pro business for the good of his health, if people wanted to waste their money on over-priced golf equipment who was he to argue? The latest transaction hadn't even required any special sales skills, a commodity of which Tobin had in abundance, but had been no less satisfying for all that.

Now his second customer of the day walked into the shop. Tobin greeted him in his trained obsequious manner. "Good morning Mr Irwin, lovely morning."

"Morning Dave. Box of balls, please," replied Irwin pleasantly.

"Maxfli, isn't it," said Tobin, reaching for a box of Dunlop Maxfli from the shelf behind him. He placed the box on the counter. "Looking forward to your round today are you, Mr Irwin?"

"Is the Pope a Catholic?" said Irwin, picking up the golf balls. "Put it on my account, would you."

"Of course, Mr Irwin. Much obliged to you. All right for tee pegs are you? I've a new type fresh in. A revolutionary new plastic developed by the NASA space programme I believe. Claimed to put ten yards on your drive, only twenty five pee."

Irwin was sold immediately. "You can't get done for twenty five pee, can you."

"Twenty do you?" suggested Tobin, intent on extracting a fiver from Irwin.

"Fine."

"Twenty it is then."

Tobin handed over the space rocket-charged tee pegs, reflected once again that there was one born every minute, watched his satisfied customer leave the shop, then turned to his new assistant Darren Lancashire, a tall, gangly seventeen-year-old with, Tobin had observed, reassuringly big feet. However the jury was still out regarding how he stacked up on the brains front.

"You will have noticed I knew which brand of golf balls Mr Irwin plays," Tobin said to his assistant. "Know your customers, Darren. Give them good service and you'll make far more money out of them than what you will ever do giving them golf lessons. Gripping their cheque, Darren, not checking their grip, that's the name of the game, that's what being a club professional is all about."

"I hear you Dave," said Darren, nodding eagerly, anxious to learn.

"I know what brand of golf ball every member of this golf club plays," Tobin went on. "Every member. Gentlemen *and* ladies. Give me the name of a member."

Darren was apologetic. "I don't know any yet Dave. Well I've only just started haven't I."

"I'll pick one then. At random. Give me a letter."

"Er...A."

"Another."

"B"

"A B. Archie Baldwin. Titleist. Another. Arnold Bradshaw. Dunlop 65. Another. Alice Bates-Weatherly. Top Flight."

"Awesome," said Darren.

"Whichever member comes into this shop for golf balls, whoever they are, even if they've only just joined, I am ready for them. Customers like you to know their preferences Darren, it makes them feel special. And it keeps my till ringing. And it isn't just their preferences in golf balls I have on tap. Sweaters, trousers, shoes, I know their tastes in those too. And their size. Archie Baldwin again. Pringle sweaters, 40 chest. Daks trousers, 38 waist, 32 inside leg. Size 9 shoes, usually Dunlop but has twice opted for Reebok."

"Awesome," said Darren.

Not awesome perhaps, but it was certainly impressive that Tobin had been able to commit to memory the golfing equipment preferences of the five hundred and twenty strong club membership. But maybe not such a big deal so far as Tobin was concerned as he was one of those fortunate people blessed with a photographic memory. This was of no great advantage to him for most things as he hardly ever exposed himself to anything worth remembering, the pages of the Daily Sport offering little else but bums and tits, as did the output of the only TV channels he watched; but insofar as being an aid to remembering precisely which member preferred what in the way of golf equipment it was obviously a huge advantage. That many people who play golf, despite it being a sport which requires nothing in the way of special clothing save for spiked shoes and a waterproof suit, find it necessary to kit themselves out in outlandish and expensive finery, only made Tobin's job even easier than it already was.

Now in his fifteenth year as a golf pro, the last four of them at Sunnymere, Tobin had left the amateur ranks of the game for the professional at the age of twenty. Like the majority of young men turning pro he had entertained high hopes of a career as a tournament professional, maybe even the European Tour if he worked hard enough at his game, but also like the majority he had eventually and almost inevitably fallen by the wayside. In Tobin's considered opinion it was chiefly because of his brains and his feet.

Shortly after turning professional, and with time on his hands after missing yet another tournament cut, he had come across an ancient golf instruction manual whilst browsing in a second hand bookshop which a fellow professional had advised him was an excellent source of porn. The tips in the book were in the main similar to those given to budding golfers in most golf instruction books, 'Keep your eye on the ball', 'Keep your head still', 'Take the club head back low and slow' etc, along with a few tips Tobin had never come across before. Some of them seemed a bit dubious to say the least, especially the advice on the correct stance to take when attempting to hit a ball that has come to rest on top of a bunker, and which if followed, Tobin felt, could only result in the golfer not only missing the ball completely but quite possibly sustaining a rupture in the process. His perusal of the book was not entirely wasted however as he did unearth one fact that turned out to be a veritable gem of wisdom; that if you wanted to be a successful golfer it was advisable to have big feet and no brains.

Unfortunately for Tobin he had small feet and a few brains, and it was the few brains he had which soon made him realise that the big feet/no brains theory, the basis of which was the contention that big feet gave the golfer a sound platform for his swing, whilst having no brains meant that he couldn't think too much about it, was an entirely sound one. Indeed, when investigating the manual's claim by analysing the results of all the golf tournaments in which he had played that year thus far he found it to be remarkably true. The golfers at the top of the leader board at the conclusion of the tournament were invariably men who were generously endowed in the feet department whilst being singularly lacking in grey matter. He soon discovered that he could pick out from amongst the field which of the starters would be the front runners, almost always including the winner amongst his selections, simply by looking at their feet and engaging them in conversation for a few minutes. Putting this information to good use he had then proceeded to make quite a bit of money betting on the outcome of the tournaments in which he took part, certainly far more money than he ever made from playing in them.

Like all rules there were exceptions to the big feet/no brains theory and occasionally a tournament would throw up a winner who had small feet and a few brains, and on one very rare occasion small feet and a lot of brains, but unfortunately Tobin was not one of them. So it eventually came to be that he gave up the soul-destroying grind of the life of a tour professional and settled for the soul-destroying grind of the life of a golf club professional who really wanted to be a tournament professional. And in doing so found his true vocation.

When he had first turned professional Tobin had boasted a handicap of one. Now, some fifteen years later, he had no idea what his handicap was. He rarely played nowadays, certainly not in any professional tournaments, and when he did play he never counted his score, but if were to hazard a guess he would have said that on a good day he might get round the Sunnymere par 70 course in a gross 76, which equates to a handicap of six. However selling was something else. Shifting golf equipment was something different altogether. He was scratch at selling. Better than scratch. Plus two or three in all probability. The superstar of club professionals, the equivalent of Tiger Woods in the tournament game. But whereas Tiger had a sweet swing and the smoothest of putting strokes

Tobin had a silver tongue and the smoothest of sales patter.

"David Holmes." said Darren.

"What?" said Tobin.

"I've remembered the name of a member," said Darren, pleased with his achievement. "David Holmes."

"David George Holmes," recited Tobin, after only a moment's thought. "Timberland sweaters, 38 chest, Pringle trousers, 40 waist, 30 inside leg, Ultra golf balls, size 10 shoes, Dexter's."

"Awesome," said Darren.

If he keeps saying 'awesome' to everything I say, thought Tobin, and with those feet, he could very well make a top tournament pro.

The second threesome of the day, Ted Dawson, Tony Elwes and George Fidler, after going through the necessary courtesies with Mr Captain, now took its place on the first tee. Dawson teed up his ball and following the time-honoured custom identified it to his playing partners. "Titleist three." He then drove off, hitting his trademark long, low fade.

"Shot," said Elwes. In the interests of camaraderie most club golfers are generous with their praise for a playing partner's shot and Elwes was no different.

"Cheers," said Dawson.

Fidler added a layer to the praise. "Never leaves you, Ted."

"Let's hope it never will, George."

Elwes then took a ball from his pocket, and, after checking that Fidler wasn't watching, exchanged a mischievous wink with Dawson, teed up his ball and said, "Top Flight four."

Fidler's ears pricked up immediately. "What?"

"Top Flight four," Elwes repeated, matter-of-fact.

"I'm playing a Top Flight four," said Fidler.

"Well so am I."

"But I always play Top Flight fours," Fidler protested. "I never play anything else. I've been playing Top Flight fours for years. Everybody knows I play Top Flight fours."

"I didn't."

Fidler found this hard to believe. "But you must have Tony. All the times we've played together?"

"Never noticed," said Elwes, airily.

"Well everybody else has noticed."

"Well I'm not everybody else, am I," said Elwes, camaraderie now having been elbowed to one side in

1 9

favour of peevishness, and with that he commenced to waggle his driver over the ball in preparation for his tee shot.

"But I haven't got anything else but Top Flight fours," Fidler complained. "It's all I ever buy, it's all I ever carry."

"Well tough titty," said Elwes, and promptly drove off. Fidler scowled his annoyance at Elwes and turned to Dawson. "Lend me a ball would you Ted."

"I've only got Titleist threes," said Dawson, "and I'm playing a Titleist three."

"You've only got Titleist threes?"

"Yes I only ever play Titleist threes."

"Since when?"

"Since I heard you only ever played Top Flight fours. I thought it was an excellent idea. Sort of personalises one."

Fidler, a man who once physically assaulted an old age pensioner who tried to push in front of him in a particularly slow Post Office queue was not a man blessed with a wealth of patience, and what little of it he had was fast running out. He turned to Elwes and held out a hand. "Lend me a ball."

"I've only got Top Flight fours," said Elwes.

At this Fidler lost his rag completely. "For fuck's sake!"

Standing no more than ten yards away from them Mr Captain could scarcely believe his ears. Fidler had used the forbidden 'F' word. In front of him. Not only used it, but shouted it, flagrantly, for all the world to hear. And on Captain's Day, of all days. *His* Captain's Day. Immediate action was called for. Mr Captain was quick in taking it. "Mr Fidler!" he remonstrated, in the sternest voice he could muster, given the shock his system had just had to contend with.

Fidler was full of apologies. "Sorry. Sorry Mr Captain, it just slipped out. Heat of the moment. Won't happen again I assure you." He cocked a thumb at Dawson and Elwes, "It wouldn't have happened at all if it hadn't been for these two clowns; they know very well I always play Top Flight fours. You'd probably have said the same thing yourself if you were in my shoes."

Mr Captain bridled at this gross insinuation. "I most certainly would not have said the same thing in your shoes," he raged. "Not in a million years. You will be required to present yourself at the next meeting of the General Committee. A week this coming Monday I believe. Eight- o-clock sharp."

"What?"

"You heard."

Not trusting himself to say another word in case he made matters worse than they already were Fidler stood fuming for a moment or so before turning on his heel and stalking off the course in the direction of the clubhouse. "I'm going for some balls," he snapped to his playing partners, over his shoulder. He could of course simply have marked his ball in order to distinguish it from Elwes's but by now he was so mad that this option didn't occur to him. And was thus instrumental in adding in no small measure to the mayhem that was to ensue that day.

Dawson and Elwes, both now grinning from ear to ear, watched him depart. Mr Captain, noticing their amusement, eyed them with suspicion. He challenged them. "Are you two deliberately trying to spoil my day?"

"Spoil your day, Mr Captain?" said Elwes, all innocence.

"I am not going to have my day spoiled by the likes of you or by anyone else."

Dawson affected surprise. "How could we be spoiling your day Mr Captain?"

"Because Fidler claimed you knew he always plays Top Flight fours, that's why. And knowing you two as I do I have no doubt you do."

Dawson now gave up all pretence of innocence. "Christ we only did it for a bit of fun, Mr Captain. It's only a laugh."

"A laugh?" echoed Mr Captain. "A laugh, Mr Dawson? Today is Captain's Day. There's nothing to laugh about."

—⁓—

Up ahead of them Arbuthnott, Chapman and Bagley had reached the first green, but not of course by the same route, as is almost always the case with the average club golf threesome. Credit must be given to Arbuthnott for getting there in the regulation two strokes, whilst both Chapman and Bagley had arrived there in the non-regulation, though more regular, three strokes. On arriving at the green, and now well out of Mr Captain's hearing, Chapman returned to the topic they had been discussing when they'd last been together on leaving the tee some ten minutes previously. "It's Captain's Day for God's sake," he railed. "Women have no right to be on the course at all on Captain's Day, let alone be entrusted with the measuring." He shook his head, bewildered. "I don't know, they put up a notice saying they don't want you to swear and then they allow women on the course at the same time as men and give you the best bloody reason in the world for swearing!"

"We can take it you won't be volunteering to do the measuring on Lady Captain's Day then, can we Gerry?" said Bagley.

"Only if it's for a wooden overcoat for one of them. Then I'd be there with my tape measure and a choice of coffins at the drop of a hat, a sarcophagus if they want one."

"Because they'll probably be expecting the gentlemen to reciprocate."

"Well they can expect all they want as far as I'm concerned," said Chapman, dismissing the whole sorry business from his mind and turning his attention to the more important matter of the forty feet left to right downhill putt he was faced with to save his par.

—w—

Frank Galloway, Mike Hanson and Richard Irwin had just left the locker room and were about to make their way to the first tee when Fidler hove into view, hurrying in the direction of the pro's shop. Hanson stopped to greet him. "George! Glad I bumped into you."

Fidler stopped and glared at him, still boiling with rage from his contretemps with Dawson and Elwes. "What?" he growled.

"The thing is my sister has bought me a dozen golf balls for my birthday and they're Top Flight fours; and you always play Top Flight fours don't you, so I was wondering if we..."

Hanson didn't get any further as without warning Fidler grabbed hold of the front of his sweater and pulled the much shorter man up onto his tiptoes. "Are you in on this with those two pillocks back there?"

"Wh...what two pillocks back where?" spluttered Hanson, struggling in a vain effort to release himself from Fidler's grip.

"Fucking Dawson and fucking Elwes."

"Careful George, Mr Captain might hear you," warned Galloway, nodding towards the first tee only some fifty yards distant.

"Fuck Mr Captain," said Fidler, having in the meantime made the decision that if he was to be hauled before the General Committee on a charge of swearing he might as well be hung for a sheep as a lamb. He tightened his grip on the struggling Hanson then thrust his face closer until their noses were almost touching, a position that did little to endear itself to Hanson as Fidler's nose had a dewdrop on the end of it which he feared might drop off and land on the new pink and grey diamond-pattern lambswool Pringle sweater Tobin had just sold him. "Well?" said Fidler.

"No. No of course not," bleated Hanson. "I don't know what you're talking about."

Fidler knew he couldn't prove anything, so despite his suspicions he released his grip on Hanson, pushed him away and stalked off in the direction of the pro's shop, not trusting himself to say another word on the subject.

"What on earth's got into George?" said Galloway, with a bemused shake of his head.

—⚓—

"Golf would be a much more enjoyable game if women had their own course," said Chapman, marking his golf ball where it had come to rest four feet short of the hole, following his approach putt.

"They have at Formby," said Arbuthnott.

"Have they really?" said Bagley, surprised. "A golf course all of their own?"

"Yes. I played there once on a day out with my company's golf society. The ladies' course is in the middle, completely encircled by the gents' course. When the gents play it's like Red Indians encircling a wagon train."

"Do they shoot arrows at them?" asked Chapman.

"I don't think they've thought of that one yet."

"I would," said Chapman, wistfully. "Poison-tipped ones."

"I don't doubt it for one moment, Gerry," said Bagley. "And throw the odd tomahawk as well no doubt."

—⚓—

When Fidler entered the pro's shop Tobin was immediately on his mettle.

"Good morning Mr Fidler. Lovely morning. Half a dozen Top Flight fours is it?"

Fidler's eyes narrowed. Could the pro be in on the conspiracy too? He wouldn't put it past him. However, unable to prove anything, he decided to give him the benefit of the doubt. "No. Half a dozen Pinnacles."

Tobin expressed surprise. "Pinnacles? But you always play Top Flight fours, Mr Fidler."

Fidler's temper, already on a very short rein, snapped again. "Well I'm not playing them today! So half a dozen fucking Pinnacles, and quick about it!"

"Yes. At once. Right away, Mr Fidler."

—⚓—

"I mean they just trivialise golf, women," Chapman went on. "What's the name of that competition they have?" He remembered it. "'Hidden Holes'. Have you ever heard of anything so stupid? You play all eighteen holes but only nine of them count. And you don't know which nine they are until it's all over. I mean what sort of a competition is that? You could have nine birdies and finish last."

"You obviously haven't taken the psychology of ladies' golf on board, Gerry," said Bagley.

"What?"

"Well it has precious little to do with the best player on the day winning. Ladies' golf is more to do with ensuring that over the course of the season as many different ladies win as possible. That's why they have lots of the type of competitions that diminish the skill factor. Flag. Three Clubs. Texas Scramble. Anything that will introduce an element of luck into the proceedings, so that even an absolute duffer at the game has some sort of a chance of winning." He chuckled as he recalled the occasion. "Someone... Irwin I think it was.... once suggested to them in all seriousness a new kind of competition they might try. 'Seventh Heaven', he called it."

"Seventh Heaven?"

"Yes, he told them it would work exactly the same as a normal medal competition except that the winner would be the lady who hits the green with her tee shot on the seventh hole, and during the walk to the green her period stops. Apparently they weren't interested."

It took only a moment for Chapman to come up with a rational reason why the suggested competition had failed to find favour with the ladies. "That's because if you had to still be having periods in order to enter ninety per cent of our lady members wouldn't qualify."

"Good point, never thought of that," said Bagley, then turned his attention to matters more important than ladies' golf, namely his putt, a tricky ten footer. After carefully lining it up he struck the putt. The ball, after narrowly missing the hole, came to rest a foot beyond. Bagley tapped it into the cup for a one over par five, a net par with his stroke.

Next to putt was Chapman. He had already looked at his putt from all angles and now placed the head of his putter behind the ball and prepared to putt, confident he would hole it.

"Some of the ladies are quite nice," said Arbuthnott, suddenly thinking of a reason for this assertion.

Chapman had a healthy dislike of lady golfers, or an unhealthy dislike, depending on your point of view, so even though he was psyched up to make his putt he could not let Arbuthnott's ridiculous contention go unchallenged. He straightened up from the Jack Nicklaus-inspired crouch he adopted as his putting style. "What?"

"The lady golfers. Some of them are quite nice."

"There is no such thing as a nice lady golfer, Arby," said Chapman with a conviction that brooked no argument. "It is a contradiction in terms."

"Mrs Stevens is nice," insisted Arbuthnott.

"Oh I agree with you there Arby," said Bagley, enthusiastically. "All the way."

Arbuthnott's claim was beyond dispute. Gloria Stevens was indeed very nice. Unless the occasion demanded otherwise, such as a funeral or a remembrance service, she always had a smile on her face, and was never less than pleasant with anyone who should cross her path. Quite well-to-do, she was generosity personified, with both her time and her money. Should any of the golf club members be taking up a collection for charity they could be sure of receiving a large donation on approaching Gloria Stevens, if she wasn't already collecting for that charity herself, which she very probably was. She did the weekly shopping for bedridden pensioners. Gave people a lift to hospital if they had no transport of their own. Drove five times a week for the Meals on Wheels Service, providing her own transport and paying for the petrol. Did two mornings a week behind the counter of the local Age Concern charity shop. Took underprivileged children on outings, entirely at her own expense. Helped out as an emergency lollipop lady when required, come rain or come shine. And she was a Samaritan. Her generosity and goodness of spirit, although legion, were surpassed by her beauty. Gloria Stevens was absolutely drop dead gorgeous. Without any doubt not only the most beautiful woman who had ever aspired to membership of the ladies' section of Sunnymere Golf Club, but the most beautiful thirty five-year-old woman that any of the members had ever seen, or hoped to see, this side of the silver screen. And with a body to die for. Well over half the male membership lusted after her, as did all nine of the club's lesbians, and she was the cause of the death, by masturbation, of the oldest life member.

"Well I don't think she's nice," said Chapman.

"Name me one thing about her that isn't nice?" challenged Arbuthnott."

"She plays golf," said Chapman.

—···—

On arriving at the first tee Galloway, Hanson and Irwin exchanged 'Good mornings' with Mr Captain, Galloway adding, "Pleasant sort of day for it."

"Brilliant, isn't it. Quite brilliant. Now don't forget the Nearest the Pin Competition at the thirteenth," said Mr Captain, then added, pointedly to Irwin. "Three of the ladies will be doing the measuring."

This was tantamount to waving a red rag at a bull as when it came to the subject of lady golfers Chapman was one of the fairer sex's staunchest supporters when compared to Irwin. There is little doubt that had there been such an organisation as the Male Chauvinist Pigs Society Irwin would have been one of their leading lights, especially if they had installed him as chairman of the Hang, Draw and Quarter all Lady Golfers Section. Now, having just received the news that ladies would be blighting the course with their presence during a gentlemen's competition Irwin's ruddy face quickly became even more red than usual. "The ladies did you say?" he spat out. "The ladies?"

Mr Captain was well aware of Irwin's opinion of lady golfers, and neither cared for the man nor his opinions, so it gave him no small pleasure to confirm what he had just said, and with relish. "Yes. The ladies, Richard."

Irwin scowled and turned away, not trusting himself to say anything further. Mr Captain could trust himself however. "And you can pull your face as much as you like. But the ladies are a very important part of this golf club."

"Especially when you're married to the one who makes the most noise," retorted Irwin, under his breath.

Mr Captain's ears pricked. "What was that? What was that you said Richard?"

"Forget it," said Irwin, and turned his attention to the watching Dawson and Elwes. "What's the hold up?"

"Fidler had to go back for some balls," explained Elwes. "I suppose we'd better let you through."

—∞—

Up ahead on the first green Arbuthnott shaped up to his putt. It wasn't an easy putt, twenty five feet or thereabouts with quite a lot of right to left borrow for the last three feet, but a putt he really fancied nevertheless.

Arbuthnott changed his putting action almost as often as he changed his socks. On average he dropped on the perfect method about once a month, only for it to become yet another imperfect method a few days later. He had tried every putting grip known to man and several known only to himself, every putting stroke from low and slow to a quick firm rap, and had executed each of the strokes with seventeen different putters, many of which he had snapped in frustration when they had let him down at a critical juncture. At the moment however he was at a stage where he had once again found the perfect method and it hadn't yet turned into another imperfect method and this, coupled with the new revolutionary titanium plated hickory shafted blade putter that Tobin had recently sold him filled him with confidence as he settled over the putt.

After the obligatory two practice putts he swung the putter head slowly back and smoothly through the ball. It kept towards its intended route, took the borrow perfectly and disappeared into the cup with a satisfying rattle. Arbuthnott punched the air. "A birdie!" He turned in triumph to his playing partners. "I told you it was going to be my day, didn't I!"

—⚏—

Even though Tobin had committed to memory the preferences in golfing equipment of every golfer in the club he had taken the precaution of backing up this information by feeding it all into his computer. He now typed in the name George Fidler, pressed the enter key, and almost immediately Fidler's details flashed up on the screen. 'Fidler, George. Sweaters, Glenmuir, 40 chest. Trousers, Nike, 36 waist, 34 inside leg. Golf balls, Top Flight four. Shoes, Reebok, size 10.'

"I knew he played Top Flight!" he exclaimed.

"Awesome," said Darren.

—⚏—

After teeing off Galloway, Hanson and Irwin were making their way up the first fairway together.

"If one of the members of a golf club dies," said Galloway, "how can you tell if it's a man or a woman just by looking at the flagpole?"

"If it's a woman the flag's at the top," said Irwin.

"Oh, you've heard it," said Galloway, disappointed.

"I thought it up," said Irwin.

—⚏—

Whilst waiting for the next threesome to tee off Mr Captain spotted, with some annoyance, that the bunker rake wasn't in its customary place next to the left-hand bunker behind the nearby eighteenth green. It brought a frown to his face. What did the green staff think they were playing at for goodness sake, didn't they know it was Captain's Day? He hoped the rake wasn't missing; that would be intolerable. It was bad enough having your ball go into a bunker in the first place, as he knew to his cost as much as anybody, without finding it nestling in a footprint left there by a previous golfer.

On walking over to investigate he discovered that the rake had been left in the bunker. Which was worse than

29

if it had been missing, if anything; for where it lay it could cause a golfer whose ball had come to rest against it, which Sod's Law almost always dictated it would, to suffer a penalty shot.

He made a note to take the head greenkeeper to task about it, and in no uncertain terms, Lord above the man was paid enough; it was his job to ensure that the golf course was presented in good order at all times and in particular at the outset of each competition, and a rake left in a bunker was simply not good enough. Especially on Captain's Day.

F Galloway (6)
M Hanson (7)
R Irwin (9)

Fidler returned to the first tee with his box of golf balls. On arriving there he took one out of the box, tore the wrapping open, savagely yanked his driver from his golf bag, teed up the ball, turned to Dawson and Elwes, treated them to the most baleful of glares and snarled, "Pinnacle two!" Then, far too quickly for his own good, and without the benefit of his customary two practice swings or even a waggle, he addressed the ball and took what can only be described as a vicious hack at it. Certainly it was not a swing you would find in any golf instruction book, although it would probably have made the pages of a seal culling instruction manual or an agricultural article on how to use a scythe. The ball left the clubface in the mother of all slices, going much farther to the right than the course did, and consequently ended up out of bounds, never to be seen again.

Dawson, Elwes and Mr Captain watched it disappear into the distance and out of view, a sight Fidler missed as he was looking, rather optimistically it must be said, up the fairway. Mr Captain, to his credit, had the good grace to turn discreetly away; however Dawson and Elwes displayed no such consideration to their playing partner, especially Elwes, who said, "You'd better take a provisional Pinnacle two George, I think you might find the one you've just taken will be out of bounds."

—⁓—

In Tobin's opinion his finest career achievement as a golf professional was not the albatross hole in one he'd had at a short three hundred and sixty eight yard par four hole, nor was it the one under par round of seventy he had once carded at Royal Lytham and St Anne's in the teeth of the same howling gale in which Nick Faldo had shot a seventy nine. Notable though these accomplishments were, the feat Tobin was most proud of and would wish to be remembered by was the occasion on which he had sold a sweater, two pairs of trousers, a hat, three golf gloves, a set of waterproofs, a pair of shoes and a new driver to one of the Sunnymere members. Golf professionals may have sold more items at a single sale, or indeed a more expensive single item, Tobin was sure, but what marked his achievement as something special was that the customer had only gone into the pro's shop for a tin of fruit pastilles.

Tobin had already instructed Darren to ensure always, after first selling the customer what they came in for, to make every effort to sell them something else, and now imparted another valuable piece of information that would be vital to his protégé if he were to enjoy any degree of success as a golf club professional.

"A tip, Darren," he said, tapping the side of his nose with his forefinger. "Spend as much time in the car park as you do on the practice ground. More time if anything. Identify each and every member with his or her car, and take notice especially of their car's registration number. Spot in particular those members whose cars have personalised number plates. If people are daft enough to shell out good money on personalised number plates they're daft enough to buy anything. These people are your prime target and main source of income. If a golfer has a personalised number plate and he comes in here for a new sweater you are not thinking acrylic, Darren, or even lambswool, you are thinking cashmere. If he requires a pair of trousers you are not looking at something in ready-made gabardine, you are looking at made-to-measure mohair. And the car park at Sunnymere Golf Club is full of personalised number plates. And my till is full of their money. Always bear that in mind."

"I'm taking notes Dave," said Darren.

Tobin now noticed Geoff Grover pass the front window on his way into the shop. He nodded in his direction to bring him to Darren's attention. "Geoff Grover. Nike sweaters, chest 44. Adidas trousers, occasionally Sunderland, 36 waist, 30 inside leg. Dunlop 65 golf balls. Size nine shoes, Enfield. Car, BMW X3, registration number GG 10."

"Awesome," said Darren.

—ᴡᴡ—

At the four hundred and twenty yard dogleg second Arbuthnott was facing a ten foot putt for another birdie. It was a much easier putt than the one he'd holed at the first, dead straight and slightly uphill, but even so he gave it just as much respect as the previous putt, acutely aware that another birdie would really set up his round, put something in the bank for the shots he would inevitably drop as his round unfolded.

Putter poised behind the ball he looked for one last time at the hole, drew his eye back to the ball, then set it in motion with a smooth stroke of his putter. Three seconds later the ball disappeared into the hole. "Get in you little beauty!" Arbuthnott shouted, punching the air again in unbridled delight, and this time adding to the celebrations by circumnavigating the hole with an animated little jig before turning to Bagley and Chapman and saying, "Are you having that? Back to back birdies! What did I tell you? What did I say?"

It was the first time Arbuthnott had ever birdied the first two holes; in fact it was only the second time he had ever birdied any two consecutive holes, and only then because on the previous occasion he had achieved one of them by holing a bunker shot after he had thinned the ball and it had hit the flagstick at about fifty miles an hour before dropping in the cup, so his joy could perhaps be excused. Not by Chapman though. "There's no need to get so excited about it Arby, you've only played two holes," he said, trying his best to diminish Arbuthnott's achievement, his partner's success already beginning to get on his wick. It didn't help that he himself had just double-bogied the same hole. "God knows what you'll do if you manage to fluke another birdie at the third, parade round the town in an open-top bus I shouldn't wonder."

"Jealousy, Gerry, pure jealousy," grinned Arbuthnott. He kissed the head of his putter, returned it to his bag, and was about to start the walk to the third tee when a thought suddenly struck him. "Where are the cameras?" he said, looking all around him.

"Cameras?" said Bagley.

"Mr Captain said he was having this filmed. This is something that should be captured on film."

"What, you making a dick of yourself?" said Chapman.

Arbuthnott smiled and enquired, pointedly, "And how many birdies have you had, pray?"

"My turn will come," said Chapman, but without a great deal of self-belief. Then, with much more conviction, "Just as sure as your turn will come for a few of your usual triple bogies."

—✕—

"Well if that is the case then that is the case, but it is most frightfully inconvenient, and you will no doubt be hearing further about this sorry affair from my solicitors, no doubt whatsoever," stormed Millicent Fridlington. She slammed down the telephone with a jolt then considered what might be done about the crisis that had just been unceremoniously dumped in her lap.

After two further phone calls she had partially retrieved the situation, but it was still of such calamitous proportions that there was nothing else for it but to inform her husband. But how?

Nowadays when needing to contact someone in a hurry most people turn to a mobile phone. However Mr Captain would not entertain one. Entirely unnecessary frivolities, he called them. He'd managed without a mobile phone for fifty two years and he was quite sure he could manage without one for whatever more years the good Lord had granted him for his stay on Earth, thank you very much. Millicent felt the same way about the infernal things. Henry had once remarked that Jesus Christ had managed to communicate with everyone without the aid of a mobile phone so there was no reason why everyone else should not be able to follow suit, and Millicent agreed with that sentiment entirely. She had mentioned Henry's erudite epithet to their son Selwyn, who did have a mobile phone, in the hope it might persuade him to get rid of it, but Selwyn had remarked, rather crudely Millicent thought, that when Jesus was on the cross he wouldn't have been able to use a mobile phone anyway. But that was Selwyn up and dressed, practical to a fault.

She could contact someone at the club by land telephone she supposed, the steward maybe, if the idle man had managed to tear himself out of bed yet, or that professional, Tobin or whatever his name was, but as Mr Captain would be in the vicinity of the first tee or maybe somewhere out on the course she could almost be there as quickly herself. But her husband would have to be informed, that much was for certain. She came to a decision; she would to go to the golf course now, much sooner than she had intended. It was a damned nuisance but there was nothing else for it.

Pausing only to pick up her handbag, Millicent set off for Sunnymere with her disastrous news.

Charlie Carter, Jack Abbott and Laurence Bradley, collectively known as the Red Arrows, were the next threesome to set off on their round that day. One had only to witness the Red Arrows leaving the tee to realise why they were known throughout the club by the same name as the world-famous Royal Air Force fighter jet display team; for Carter habitually hit everything to the left, Abbott hit everything to the right, and Bradley hit everything straight down the middle. Consequently when they stepped off the front of the tee to make their way up the fairway Carter habitually broke to his left, Abbott broke to his right, whilst Bradley proceeded dead straight ahead, and as they did this simultaneously it looked for all the world like the Red Arrows display team peeling off in their world-renowned sunburst manoeuvre. This didn't always happen of course, they were human after all, and even a tournament professional cannot guarantee to hit every shot the same, much less a long handicapper, but it happened more often than not and certainly enough to make it noteworthy.

The Red Arrows had accepted their nickname with good grace and now, having borne the appellation for the twenty or so years they had been playing together, were quite proud of it, indeed rejoiced in it, so much so that they had taken to wearing matching red sweaters, a refinement that had the effect of making them look even more like the real Red Arrows when they burst forth from the tee. Carter, the more adventurous of the three, had once suggested that their ensemble include red trousers too but the other two members of the trio had demurred on the grounds of over-egging the custard.

36

The only hiccup they had experienced in their career had occurred soon after they had been christened the Red Arrows. When news of their fame had spread throughout the club they had started to attract an audience, eager to see the display, and especially so at the outset of their round, as the first tee was overlooked by the clubhouse, which provided a convenient auditorium from which to view the grand spectacle. Seats on the veranda were at a premium. In fact it had been known for some members of the club who were not playing golf that day, and had no other call to be at the club, to drop in with the express purpose of witnessing the phenomenon.

The first time the Red Arrows ever drew spectators, and anxious not to let their audience down, and after Carter had already hit his tee shot to the left, Abbott had then deliberately tried to hit his ball to the right, but in doing so had only succeeded in hitting it to the left, where it joined Carter's ball in a bunker, much to his great surprise and disappointment, and the disappointment of the watching gallery. Bradley had then hit his tee shot straight down the middle as usual with the result that instead of having one ball to the left, one ball to the right and one ball down the middle, they had two balls to the left and one ball down the middle, and consequently when the Red Arrows left the tee the sunburst effect was only half as spectacular. Abbott had learned his lesson and from that day on always tried to hit the ball straight, thus almost guaranteeing that it went to the right, and the display returned to normal.

Anyone who is at all familiar with the game of golf would suspect that Bradley, always down the middle, would be by far the better golfer of the three, but in fact he was marginally the worst. The main reason for this was that although he invariably hit the ball straight he never succeeded in hitting it very far, whereas Carter and Abbott were both powerful strikers of the ball. After their tee shots Bradley's ball would be typically straight down the middle and about a hundred and eighty yards distant, whilst Carter's ball would be about two hundred and thirty yards distant but forty yards to the left and

Abbott's ball a similar distance to the right, thus leaving all three of them approximately the same distance from the green. After their approach shots, and also on Sunnymere's five short par three holes, Bradley's ball would either end up on the green, or more usually, due to his lack of hitting power, some way short of it, whilst the balls of Carter and Abbott would more than likely be about pin high forty yards to the left and right of the green respectively, thus giving Bradley a distinct advantage. However this advantage was negated by Bradley's skill with the putter, which was as non-existent as his playing partners' skill off the tee.

The Red Arrows now drove off. The sunburst followed. Another breathtaking display was underway.

—◇—

Grover entered the pro's shop. Despite being the proud owner of a personalised number plate Grover wasn't one of Tobin's best customers, perhaps being the exception that proves the rule, but he was a steady enough client nevertheless, a couple of new sweaters and pair of new trousers a year man and perhaps new golf shoes every two or three years, so well worth buttering up. Tobin loaded his butter knife and started spreading generously. "And a very good morning to you, Mr Grover," he said. "Lovely day for it. You must fancy your chances more than somewhat today, my word must you; I was watching you play down the ninth and up the tenth the other day and your swing looked to be in very fine fettle, I've never seen you swinging better, put me in mind of Sergio Garcia but not so willowy. So how can I be of assistance to you? The new Nike range is in, they have some really nice sweaters in their latest collection, better even than is usually the case, and that's saying something."

"Well I sincerely hope they're better than the last one I bought off you," said Grover, snootily. "Because it was absolute rubbish."

This wasn't the response Tobin had been expecting. 'Let me have a look at them would you?' or 'Have you anything in blue?' or, more hopefully, 'I'll take half a dozen' being more the sort of reply he'd been looking for, so Grover's complaint threw him a little. "Pardon, Mr Grover?" he said, after getting over the initial shock.

"Well it titted, didn't it."

"Titted?"

"Titted," repeated Grover. The re-iteration of the un-familiar word left Tobin none the wiser judging by the puzzled expression on his face. Grover elucidated. "My wife borrowed it. When I got it back from her she wasn't in it any more but it looked like her tits still were. Completely ruined it of course, there's no way I can ever wear it again."

The last thing Tobin wanted was a dissatisfied customer. In his experience a dissatisfied customer very often became an ex-customer. Which is why he didn't suggest the first thing to come into his head – that a possible way round the problem was to make a gift of the sweater to Mrs Grover, seeing as how it now had room for her tits in it – but instead employed a little discretion in an attempt to worm his way back into Grover's good books. "Er...actually, and I'm sure you won't mind me mentioning this Mr Grover, but I don't think ladies are supposed to wear men's sweaters," he said, suitably unctuous, before continuing with the learning. "You see ladies sweaters are designed differently than men's; they're a different shape, to accommodate the breasts. Whereas men's sweaters are...."

Grover broke in, now getting quite angry about it. "Are you telling me a sweater I paid you the best part of fifty quid for is of such poor quality that it won't revert back to its former shape just because it's had a pair of tits in it for a couple of hours?"

"Well..." said Tobin, searching for but not immediately finding another excuse for what had happened to the sweater.

Grover didn't give him any more time to come up with one. "Half a dozen Dunlop 65s, if you please!"

"Yes Mr Grover. At once," said Tobin, quickly handing Grover a box of Dunlop 65s, then, in another effort to repair the damage. "On the house, of course."

39

"I should bloody well think so too," said Grover, taking the box and making for the door.

—⁓—

Fidler drove off the second tee. Taking a triple bogey seven at the first, including the two shot penalty he'd incurred for hitting his first ball out of bounds, had done nothing to improve his temper. However during the short walk from the first green to the second tee he had managed to calm himself down a little, and this time made a much better fist of his drive, the ball on this occasion not veering off line by about a hundred yards to the right and sailing out of bounds, but veering only fifty yards to the right and sailing out of bounds.

"Shit!" he shouted, as he watched it disappear into the ether and over the perimeter wall.

"I think another Pinnacle two might be in order, George," Elwes observed, drily.

—⁓—

On the third green Arbuthnott had just missed a four-footer to save his par, his ball unfortunately just lipping out of the cup.

"Oh hard luck, Arby," Bagley commiserated.

"The rot's setting in I see," observed Chapman, commiseration for Arbuthnott not being on his agenda. "As I seem to remember remarking it would not too long ago."

Arbuthnott retrieved his ball from the can, not too disappointed. "Well it's only a bogey," he consoled himself, "I'm still one under gross."

"It's early days," said Chapman portentously, then started the lengthy business of lining up the putt for his par.

Arbuthnott however was not about to have his convictions shaken by Chapman's sniping. "It's my day, Gerry. I've told you. It's fated. It is written."

"We'll see, we'll see."

The third green at Sunnymere is quite elevated and steeply sloped from back to front. Anyone looking at it from the fairway, or even looking from the front of the green to the back, would see nothing beyond it but the infinity of the sky. Under normal circumstances. Now however, just as Chapman was about to putt, a view which had remained unchanged since the course was laid out over a hundred years earlier was instantly transformed when a large helicopter suddenly erupted from behind the green and commenced to hover some twenty feet overhead, propellers whirling, jet engines howling, a cameraman hanging precariously out of the doorway filming the action on the green.

"Fuck me!" said Chapman, dropping his putter in alarm.

Bagley cupped a hand to his mouth and mischievously called in the direction of the first tee, "Chapman's swearing again, Mr Captain!"

—᠁—

Grover emerged from the pro's shop where his playing partners for that day, Trevor Armitage and Gerard Stocks, had been waiting patiently for him outside the door whilst discussing their relative chances of lifting the silverware that day, Armitage hopeful, Stocks less so.

Grover gaily tossed the box of Dunlop 65s up in the air, and caught it. "He'll believe anything, that pro," he smiled.

The story of what had happened to his sweater was in fact just that, a story, a lie. Grover had thought for some time that Tobin was just a little bit too cocky with all his sales patter and needed to be taken down a peg or two and the tale of the titted sweater was his way of doing it. That he'd gained a free box of golf balls into the bargain was a bonus.

"What's that?" said Stocks.

"Nothing," replied Grover. But it was far from nothing, and would prove to be as instrumental in spoiling Mr Captain's Day as Fidler's habit of always playing Top Flight four balls.

9.10 a.m.
R Garland (6)
T Harris (9)
J Ifield (9)

"Good morning gentlemen," said Mr Captain, welcoming to the first tee the fourth threesome that morning. It comprised of Robin Garland, who was the vice captain this year, and his playing partners Terry Harris and Justin Ifield.

"Well at the moment it is," said Ifield, in his naturally gloomy voice.

"Pardon? What was that you said, Justin?" said Mr Captain, knowing what Ifield had said but not why he had said it.

"Well it's going to start raining by eleven-o-clock, isn't it."

"Raining?" This was news to Mr Captain and not news he wanted to hear. "Are you sure?"

"Cats and dogs. Stair rods. Noah's Ark proportions, I believe. Hope you've got your waterproofs with you Mr Captain, you're certainly going to need them. And a pair of wellington boots. Maybe a rowing boat would help, and a couple of distress flares."

Mr Captain looked anxiously at the sky. It was quite blue. "But there isn't a cloud in the sky."

"Well I'm only telling you what Fred the Weatherman said on the television last night" said Ifield. "And I swear by him. Well I would if I was allowed to swear," he added, artfully, then went on, "A warm night for the time of the year, minimum temperature fourteen degrees, followed by a promising start to the morning, but by eleven- o-clock this will have deteriorated, dark storm clouds quickly forming, leading to torrential non-stop rain for the rest of the day." His gloomy voice made the forecast sound even gloomier than he had painted it. "Fine tomorrow," he concluded, adding insult to injury.

42

Mr Captain checked the sky again. It looked as though it would never rain again, never mind in less than two hours' time. But if it had been on the television weather forecast? They could be wrong of course, but they weren't all that far out usually, and this wasn't Michael Fish who had done the forecasting but Fred the Weatherman whose meteorological predictions he knew to be reasonably reliable. "You are quite sure about this are you, Justin?" he asked Ifield again.

Ifield nodded. "Well that's what Fred said. And I've never known him to be wrong yet. Especially where rain is concerned. It'll be coming down in buckets, no doubt about it."

"And they do say there's only two things you can be absolutely certain of coming down," said Harris, knowledgeably. "Rain, and knickers on a honeymoon."

Mr Captain disliked crude talk almost as much as he disliked swearing but was so concerned by Ifield's weather prediction that he didn't even bat an eyelid at Harris's coarseness, far less pull him up about it.

— ∭ —

Not only is golf one of the most expensive sports to take up, it is one of the most difficult to play. It is possible, indeed usual, to pay over a thousand pounds to join a golf club, a further thousand pounds in annual membership fees, in excess of five hundred pounds for a set of clubs and a similar amount in competition fees and sundry expenses, and in return for such a high outlay receive nothing for it but utter frustration, if not humiliation. It is some sort of consolation therefore, and an advantage which golf holds over most other sports, that it is a game which is almost always played in pleasant surroundings. Not for golf the bare enclosed environs of a squash court or the monotony of an endless running track, a muddy rugby pitch or the stark tiled surfaces of a swimming pool. No, by and large the amphitheatre in which the golfer plays his sport is of gently rolling pastures or links land, trees and bushes of every known variety lining the fairways as they wind their broad green swathe from tee to green, with perhaps some colourful clumps of gorse and heather here and there, enhanced by little swales and hillocks, maybe a small stream criss-crossing the fairway at various points as it threads a path through the course, with very often a lake or two.

An added attraction is that when a golfer goes about his golf he is much nearer to nature than is the participator in most other sports. There are birds to see and hear, ducks, geese, pied wagtails, jays, kingfishers; there are small mammals to observe, squirrels, rabbits, stoats, weasels, maybe a fox or a deer if one is lucky; there are insects, dragonflies, butterflies and moths; and there are wild flowers and colourful shrubs to see and smell. And as the golfer proceeds on his way through the course, from driving off at the first tee until putting out on the eighteenth green, he can continually drink from his surroundings, take sustenance from them, so that even if he is having a bad day as far as the golf is concerned his journey will not have been a complete waste of time. Not without good reason did Mark Twain once comment that golf is a good walk spoilt.

Sunnymere Golf Club was especially blessed. A member of a visiting party once remarked that he always enjoyed playing there as the course was so picturesque that he didn't really mind how well or badly he played. Located in the Derbyshire Dales, itself considered by many to be the brightest jewel in England's crown, not only was the golf course itself set in beautiful countryside but it was surrounded by even more beautiful countryside, and as far as the eye could see.

The area around Sunnymere attracted many visitors, and at 9.10 a.m. on Captain's Day it had attracted two such visitors to the small copse just to the left of the limestone boundary wall bordering the second fairway. They were two young lovers, Dean Shawcross and his girlfriend Gemma Higginbottom, he eighteen years old, she a year younger. Who at the moment were loving. At least that's what Gemma called it. Dean called it getting his end away. And Gemma was loving, and Dean was getting his end away, as naked as the day they were born.

In the nuddy as Gemma called it. Strip bollock naked as Dean called it.

Their coupling in the woods was born of necessity rather than any desire to fornicate al fresco. He wanted to make love, she wanted to make love, but there was nowhere for them to make it. He shared a bedroom with two older and inconsiderate brothers, who, far from keeping out of the way for an hour or so in order that he and his girlfriend might have the privacy of the bedroom to themselves, were far more likely to burst in on their lovemaking just for the fun of it; she had her own bedroom, but along with it a very strict mother who would 'have none of that sort of thing going off under my roof, young lady'. Whenever the two young lovers had the opportunity to be together it seemed that there was always somebody in Dean's house and always somebody in Gemma's house. This was especially true of Gemma's house if Dean happened to be in it, Gemma's mother making sure of that. So they made love wherever they could, and today they were making it in the copse by the second fairway at Sunnymere; and going at it as if their lives depended on it.

—⁓—

Yet another advantage that golf enjoys over most other sports is that it provides almost constant opportunity to engage one's playing partners in conversation, particularly on the walk between shots. (This maxim applies only to the better golfers who hit the ball reasonably straight, and not of course to the poorer golfers who, once they have left the tee, rarely meet up again until they reach the green.)

During the game of football conversation is hardly viable, most talk on the field of play being limited to calling for the ball, shouting 'Our ball!' to the referee whenever the ball goes over a by-line whether the player thinks it is his team's ball or not, telling a fellow team member to get his bleeding finger out, and calling a member of the opposing team a dirty bastard who will very soon be getting what's fucking coming to him. Tennis too has few possibilities for a pleasant chat; the players are rarely within hearing distance of each other except when they're both at the net, and on those occasions they are far too busy trying to hit the ball back to exchange the latest gossip. As for boxing, well one certainly gets close enough to the man one is fighting to have a natter, as Muhammad Ali has proved with great wit, but both the wearing of a gum shield and the fact that you are constantly being batted round the head by your opponent does little to encourage any conversation other than the odd cry of "Ow, that hurt!"

Golf however throws up many chances for a chat and as Garland, Harris and Ifield were making their way up the first fairway together they were taking the first such opportunity the morning's round had thrown up.

"I saw the weather forecast last night," remarked Harris, to Ifield. "The man didn't say anything about the weather turning; on the contrary he said it was going to be bright and sunny all day."

"It is."

"Then why did you tell Mr Captain it was going to rain?"

"To give the self-satisfied prick something to worry about," said Ifield. He smiled. "We don't want him enjoying his Captain's Day too much, do we."

"How much longer do we have to put up with the tit for anyway?" said Harris.

"Another nine months," said Garland, sadly.

"Christ, is it that long? You've got time to have a baby in nine months."

"I think I'd rather have a baby than stick another nine months of Henry Fridlington," said Harris. "I could put up with all the morning sickness and sore nipples and eating coal sandwiches."

"Me too," said Garland. "I'm not too sure about the pain of giving birth though," he added, after a moment's reflection.

"That's exaggerated, Mr Vice," said Ifield. "Women make out it's a lot worse than it is so you'll feel sorry for them."

"I think you could be right there," agreed Harris. "My grandmother used to say giving birth is only like having a good shit. Mind you, she had fourteen children so by the time she had the fourteenth it probably was like having a good shit."

"My grandmother actually gave birth to my Uncle Reg when she *was* having a shit," said Ifield. "So she'd know for definite."

"When she was having a shit?"

"Yes. Apparently she went to the bathroom for a shit, squeezed like you do, and out came my Uncle Reg along with the shit. She had to haul him out of the lavatory pan by the umbilical cord, smartish. It was only that that stopped him drowning. They were thinking of calling him Lucky before they settled for Reg."

They walked silently for a while, possibly marvelling at the twin miracles of childbirth and having a good shit, before Garland thought of another topic he felt worthy of giving an airing.

"When I take over as Mr Captain next year I'm going to have a compulsory beer tent. Every player in my Captain's Day competition will have to get a minimum of four pints of bitter or six shorts down him before he's allowed to continue his round."

"And no ladies," said Harris.

"Well only if you can manage one after the four pints of bitter or six shorts."

All three of them laughed hugely at Garland's chauvinistic aside, then Ifield produced a packet of sweets from his golf bag and offered them round. "Fancy a mint, Mr Vice?"

"Do bears shit in the woods?" said Garland, helping himself to a mint.

—⁓—

True to form Red Arrow member Charlie Carter sprayed his tee shot at the second hole fifty yards to the left, whereupon his ball came to rest ten yards or so into the light rough, close by the wall bordering the fairway. He had almost reached the errant sphere and was wondering what sort of a lie he would find it in when an unfamiliar noise to his right captured his attention. He peered over the wall, down into the little copse, and immediately saw the reason for the strange noise. It was a couple making love, the noise being unfamiliar to him as it had been a long time since Carter, now in his early seventies, had had the pleasure of making love, and had completely forgotten what it sounded like.

In the Year of Our Lord 2009 the sight of a couple copulating is quite commonplace. One has only to switch on the television set or visit a cinema and it's bound to appear sooner or later, probably sooner, but the sight of two fit-looking young people making love in the flesh, and with such joyful abandon, was not something one saw every day. A considerate man, Carter immediately thought that his playing partners might like to view the spectacle too. Consequently he waved to attract the attention of Bradley and Abbott, some fifty and a hundred yards away respectively, and having gained their attention beckoned them over to join him. They made their way over and as they drew nearer to him Carter put a finger to his lips as a warning for them to keep quiet. Once they had joined him, and after Abbott had remarked that he had never been on this side of the course before and how nice it was, especially the rhododendron bushes, Carter drew their attention to Dean and Gemma, who were still going at it like knives.

Abbott was immediately in awe at the sight set out before him. "Jesus, watch the bugger go," he whispered.

"Like the piston on an 0-6-0 shunter," said Bradley, a trainspotting anorak, keeping his voice down.

"And not a stitch on," said Carter, like Bradley keeping his voice down, but not making any attempt to keep the excitement out of it. "Naked as nature intended!"

"Certainly brings back memories," said Abbott, who at seventy six was even older than Carter.

"No age either, by the look of them," observed Bradley. "When I was that age I hadn't even had a feel of a titty except through a duffel coat, and even then she made me wear gloves."

"Yes, we were born fifty years too soon lads," said Carter, wistfully. "I even missed out on the Swinging Sixties by ten years."

"Me too," said Abbott. "But even the Swinging Sixties didn't swing anything like as much as things do nowadays."

They looked down fondly and a little jealously on the coupling couple, for it really was a sight to behold. For the act of love is only rarely engaged in by people blessed with such slim, toned and tanned bodies as those of Dean and Gemma, more typically being performed by couples who carry a generous surplus of white flesh, with the result that the union resembles nothing more than a third-rate wrestling bout with added juices, rather than the thing of beauty it was with the two young lovers.

The three watched a little longer, then Carter said, "Come on, we'd best be off, it's making me feel randy and that won't do my game any good at all, I don't know if I'd be able to putt with a hard on."

"It might help you to keep your head still," said Abbott.

"It wouldn't help him to keep his arse still," said Bradley.

And that would have been that. But just at that moment, and accompanied by a joyous moan from Gemma and an enormous grunt from Dean, the couple reached their climax together, and as they came Gemma opened her eyes. And over Dean's shoulder saw the Red Arrows gazing down at her. She shrieked at least as loud as Fay Wray had when she first set eyes on King Kong, at the same time pointing an accusing finger at them. Concerned for his lover, Dean turned to look at the cause of her anguish. Seeing the three accidental voyeurs he screamed at the top of his voice, "You fucking dirty old men!" at the same time uncoupling himself from his amour and turning to face them.

"Bloody hell!" said Carter.

"Shit!" said Abbott.

"Bloody shit!" said Bradley

Rage contorting his handsome young features Dean sprang to his feet, shook his fist at the Red Arrows and warned, "Just wait till I get my hands on you, you dirty old buggers!"

Dean was a big lad for his age, six feet two inches tall and well-built, with wide shoulders and a great six-pack, a fact already noted by Carter, hence his anxiety to make himself scarce and with due haste. None of the Red Arrows were anything like so well-built, and if any of them had ever had a six-pack it had long since regressed into a one-pack, and a very large one-pack at that where Abbott and Carter were concerned.

Dean now began to make his way menacingly towards them, and as he showed no signs of letting the wall between them, or his nudity, halt his progress, the Red Arrows knew that the only option open to them was to run for it; to scramble, in Red Arrows parlance. So as one they turned and fled, and on hitting the fairway slipped quite naturally into full Red Arrows mode and peeled off in a sunburst, Abbott heading to his right, Carter to his left, Bradley straight ahead, each of them running as fast as their ancient legs could carry them, which, given that between them they shared an arthritic hip, two arthritic knees, a bad back, a fallen arch, a bunion and two in-growing toenails, wasn't very fast at all. Dean, having leapt over the wall and observed that the Red Arrows had split up, was faced with the decision of which one of them to chase. Abbott, the fattest of the three, looked to him to be making the heaviest weather of his flight. Dean targeted him and gave chase.

—⁓—

Mrs Quayle, Mrs Rattray and Mrs Salinas, the three ladies entrusted with the task of measuring in the Nearest the Pin competition, were making their way to the thirteenth green. All the ladies were in their fifties. Mrs Quayle was a quite short, petite woman, whereas Mrs Rattray and Mrs Salinas carried the more generous build more usually associated with lady golfers of their years. Mrs Rattray was especially well-upholstered, and the possessor of two very large breasts and a no less impressively proportioned behind. She had wisely made use of her twin physical attributes in developing her quite individual golf swing, which was a thing of no little power, 'All buttocks, bust and thrust' as one of the gentlemen members had once remarked, and perhaps because of it she boasted a handicap of sixteen, well above average for a lady golfer.

The three ladies were dressed in the pastel shades beloved of all lady golfers, and not a few male golfers, skirts for Mrs Rattray and Mrs Salinas, trousers for Mrs Quayle (who liked to keep her legs covered up whenever possible due to the triple afflictions of cellulite, varicose veins and vanity), whilst each had chosen different styles of headgear for the occasion, Mrs Quayle sporting a red and white striped baseball cap, Mrs Rattray a yellow sun visor, whilst Mrs Salinas had plumped for a flower-patterned floppy sun hat. Each of the ladies carried a folding chair in one hand and a shopping bag in the other. As they ambled slowly along the side of the second fairway it looked for all the world as though they were setting out on a summer picnic, which indeed they were, as all three of them viewed their measuring duties in the Nearest the Pin competition as a very poor second to feasting later on their packed lunch of Mrs Rattray's special cucumber and smoked salmon sandwiches, Mrs Quayle's delicious homemade quiche and Mrs Salinas's fairy cakes. Washed down with Darjeeling tea from Mrs Quayle's flask. Mrs Salinas's flask carried morning coffee for the ladies, Mrs Rattray's a refreshing iced fruit cup. On the way to their destination the ladies chatted and chattered.

"Well I don't think you can beat Marks and Spencers for curtains," said Mrs Quayle.

"Debenhams are very good," offered Mrs Rattray.

"Oh Debenhams are excellent," agreed Mrs Salinas. "I bought my dining room curtains from Debenhams."

"The ones with the plates on?" asked Mrs Quayle.

"No, that's my kitchen curtains. They were from Littlewoods. No, my Debenhams curtains have teapots on them."

"But of course they do!"

"But then Debenhams don't sell food, do they," observed Mrs Rattray. "So if you're shopping for food *and* curtains you're better off going to Marks, as you can get both at the same time. Whereas if you go to Debenhams you can't do that."

"Or Primark," said Mrs Quayle.

"Or Primark," agreed Mrs Rattray.

Now, emerging from behind a small hillock on the edge of the fairway, Abbott, running as though his very life depended on it, which may well have been the case, pursued some thirty yards behind by Dean Shawcross, came into view heading in the direction of the clubhouse and the exit from the course. The spectacle of a fat red-faced pensioner being chased by a completely naked eighteen-year-old is a sight not often seen on a golf course, but far from stopping them in their tracks the ladies didn't even break stride.

"Good morning, gentlemen," Mrs Salinas trilled, before continuing with more important matters. "British Home Stores are quite good for curtains, too," she opined, switching in a trice the whole of her attention back to Mrs Quayle and Mrs Rattray and the soft furnishings retail industry.

"And light fittings," said Mrs Quayle, whose attention had never left the soft furnishings retail industry, despite seeing a young man in full frontal mode.

"Oh yes, their light fittings are excellent," agreed Mrs Rattray. "They're the absolute best for light fittings, I got my uplighter from British Home Stores. They do a very tasty prawn sandwich too, excellent mayonnaise."

—⁂—

Mr Captain was making his way back to the first tee after having paid a visit to the beer tent. Drinks wouldn't be served until the first threesome of Arbuthnott, Bagley and Chapman arrived there after completing the ninth hole, in around an hour's time, but he had wanted to assure himself that everything there was shipshape and Bristol fashion. After all, it would be the venue where he would be entertaining no less a personage than His Worshipful the Lord Mayor of Sunnymere, who was scheduled to arrive at eleven twenty, and he didn't want to risk anything being less than perfect for the occasion. If Captain's Day was the highlight of Mr Captain's year of office then the Mayoral visit would be the *piece de resistance* of his Captain's Day.

There had never before been a Mayoral visit in the entire one hundred and ten year history of Sunnymere Golf Club. Mr Captain had checked. There had been members of the golf club who had been Lord Mayor, indeed one of them had been Lord Mayor at the same time as he had been captain, but that was an altogether different thing, so the first ever Mayoral visit would be a huge feather in his cap. His Worship would be paying only a flying visit, true, between opening the new council-funded skateboard & tattooing centre and closing the council-run old folks' home due to lack of resources, but he would of course be returning in the evening to be guest of honour at the dinner and dance.

Mr Captain had his wife to thank for coming up with the idea. Millicent was a collector of miniature china figurines, and as such was a regular customer of China Times, a gift shop in the town which sold delicate porcelain at indelicate prices. The shop was owned and run by Edna Burroughs, the wife of the current Lord Mayor. Both Millicent and Edna were members of the local bridge circle and over the years had become, if not close friends, then friendly acquaintances. So much so that when Mr Captain had expressed a desire for something that would make his Captain's Day special, something out of the ordinary that would make it stand out from other Captain's Days, Millicent had thought immediately of her connection with the wife of the Lord Mayor, and through her with the Lord Mayor himself. Within twenty four hours, which was as long as it took for Millicent to purchase five hundred pounds worth of porcelain from China Times and for news of her purchase to reach the ears of the Lord Mayor via his wife, the Mayoral visit had been arranged. Mr Captain had been doubly pleased. Not only would the visit of the Lord Mayor bring him much esteem, but it could very well lead to he himself becoming

Lord Mayor one day, an ambition he had been harbouring for quite some time.

To become Lord Mayor would of course first necessitate his being voted onto the local town council, which until now had been the stumbling block in the road to his ambitions. So far as Mr Captain could see there were two ways which would ensure that enough of the electorate voted for you to give you a seat on the town council; by becoming a popular member of the community through being a do-gooder who worked hard for those people less fortunate than himself, and who championed the causes of the underdog; or by being recognised as a natural leader of men.

Mr Captain knew that if he were to remain true to his beliefs he could never become a councillor by the former method. He didn't believe in putting himself out for others, quite the opposite, he had always held the opinion that if you worked hard for people less fortunate than yourself they would simply take advantage of you, when what they should be doing is asking themselves why they were less fortunate than you in the first place and damn well doing something about it. As for championing the underdog, let the underdog get up off his idle backside and champion himself if he wanted to make something of himself. However, now that he was captain of the local golf club, and especially now it would be seen by all and sundry that he was a friend of the present Lord Mayor, who happened to be a man with whom he shared the same political leanings, there was every chance he might be recognised as a natural leader of men.

It certainly wouldn't be for want of trying, that much was for sure. The local newspaper had been informed of the occasion and had agreed to send along a reporter and photographer to cover the event, and the local radio station had promised to send someone along to report on the day's proceedings. After that it would simply be a matter of getting the Lord Mayor to endorse his nomination for the next local elections, and he would be on his way.

—〜—

Having hit their drives at the par four fourth, Elwes and Dawson were standing at the side of the tee waiting for Fidler to tee off.

"Will you be calling in at the nineteenth for a couple later?" asked Elwes of Dawson.

"Does the Pope shit in the woods?" said Dawson.

"Quiet!" barked Fidler. "On the tee!"

Dawson and Elwes stopped talking, respecting their playing partner's right to total silence while he was making his shot. Fidler hit his drive and anxiously watched the flight of his ball. His tee shot at the previous hole had been much better, more like one of his usual drives, finding the fairway for the first time that day, but this time his drive was just as wild as the first two had been. On this occasion however his ball didn't go out of bounds, but only because a copse of tall trees bordering the fairway stopped it from doing so. The ball ricocheted from tree to tree half a dozen times, much like a ball in a pinball machine. Whenever this happens - as it often does in club golf - and if you are in luck, the last ricochet can deposit the ball on the fairway. Fidler was not in luck and his ball came to rest somewhere, he knew not where, deep in the trees. Dawson and Elwes cringed as they waited for the expected outburst from Fidler. They didn't have long to wait.

"This is you two, all this," Fidler raged. "This is your doing. I always hit everything dead straight when I play Top Flight fours!"

"Yes, I'm hitting Top Flight fours pretty straight myself," said Elwes agreeably, then added, "But then of course I usually am fairly straight."

"*I'd* be fairly fucking straight if I was playing Top Flight fours," Fidler ranted.

"Oh come on George, you can't blame your wild hitting on the type of ball you're using," scoffed Dawson.

"It is the bloody ball! It is! I'm as straight as a die with Top Flight fours."

Elwes goaded Fidler further. "It's a bad workman who blames his tools."

"It's you two tools who I'm blaming. As well as the bloody ball."

"You'd better play a provisional," Elwes advised. He took a ball from his golf bag. "Here, try one of my Top Flight fours since you hit them so straight." He produced a felt tip pen. "I'll mark it so it can't get mixed up with my Top Flight four."

"There's no chance of that happening Tony," said Dawson, as adept at stirring as was Elwes. "Your ball will be the one on the fairway."

Fidler, just about managing to stop himself rising to the bait, accepted the marked ball from Elwes. After taking a few seconds to compose himself, and taking great care in taking up his stance and lining himself up with the intended target, he finally settled over the ball. He was just about to start taking the club head back when the helicopter suddenly appeared as if from nowhere, crossing the fairway some hundred yards ahead, at a height of about thirty feet. Fidler, having been warned by Mr Captain about the helicopter, was not surprised by its appearance, and although annoyed, simply stood back and watched it until it had disappeared from view, then went through the whole setting up procedure again, if anything even more meticulously than before. Then he drove off. This time the ball hit the fairway, plumb centre. Unfortunately, due to a violent hook, it wasn't the fairway of the hole he was playing but the fairway of the eleventh hole, which ran parallel to the fourth.

"Shit!" said Fidler.

"Maybe you could get the helicopter pilot to spot for you?" suggested Elwes.

Fidler fixed him. "And maybe you could keep your fucking great trap of a mouth shut."

—⚹—

Mr Captain arrived back at the first tee just in time to welcome the next three ball of Trevor Armitage, Gerard Stock and George Grover.

"How's it all going then, Mr Captain?" said Grover. "Your Captain's Day?"

"Oh excellent, George. Quite excellent. All I could have hoped for. I had to put Richard Irwin in his place about the ladies, but apart from that there has not been even a minor blip."

No sooner had the words left Mr Captain's mouth than the first minor blip arrived in the shape of Abbott. Quickly followed by a major blip in the shape of the naked Dean Shawcross. Fortunately for Abbott, with Dean by now almost upon him, his route off the golf course took him across the gravel path that led from the clubhouse to the first tee, and when Dean followed him onto the path the sharp gravel chippings dug into his feet and immediately brought him hopping to a stop.

In the meantime Abbott sped on. Dean saw there was nothing for it but to abandon the chase and contented himself with shaking a fist after Abbott and shouting, "Wait till I get my hands on you, I'll tear you apart you dirty old get!" Then he noticed Mr Captain and the others, who were staring at him, open-mouthed. He returned their stares with a hostile glare and said, "And who the hell do you lot think you are staring at?"

Mr Captain could scarcely believe his eyes. A naked man on the golf course? On Captain's Day? He was apoplectic, completely lost for words. Observing that Dean had turned and was about to start making his way back from whence he came he just about managed to find a few. "What...what is the meaning of this?" he demanded.

"Oh fuck off, Grandad," said Dean, and started to depart the scene.

Mr Captain was outraged. "Come back here at once!" he called after him. "This instant. Do you hear me? This is private land. You are trespassing."

Dean had obviously heard Mr Captain as he now put his hand behind his back, his fingers formed in a V-sign, a pictorial reiteration of his words of a moment ago, but continued on his way in silence and without pause.

"I said come back here!" Mr Captain turned to the others, his face getting more red and outraged by the second. "Did you see that?" he said, still scarcely able to credit what he had just witnessed. "Did you see that.... that lout?"

"Yes," said Grover. "A thoroughly bad show, Mr Captain. I hope it hasn't spoiled your day."

"It's spoiled my day," said Armitage. "Did you see the dick on him?"

Grover grimaced. "I hope you're not going to start going on about dicks again, Trevor," he said with a sigh. "You're always going on about the size of people's dicks."

"Who is?" said Armitage.

Jason Fearon needed money. The trouble was that to a boy of only thirteen years of age the opportunities for making money are severely limited. Running errands for neighbours brought in a little bit, but the sort of neighbours who needed errands running for them, the old and the infirm, usually had little money to spare to shell out for errands to be run for them, so any income he made from such ventures was never more than a trickle, whilst Jason's needs were more in the nature of a stream or small river.

Eventually he would be able to get a job as a paper boy or help out in a shop or washing up in a pub's kitchen or something, but you had to be fourteen before they let you do that. This restriction seemed grossly unfair to Jason as it seemed to him that the needs of a thirteen-year-old boy and a fourteen-year-old boy were more or less the same - new video games, CDs, football boots, mobile phone, I-Pod, whatever. He had his weekly pocket money of course, five pounds, plus two pounds he got from his nana for cleaning her downstairs windows every time she felt they needed doing, which wasn't often enough as far as Jason was concerned, but five pounds and the occasional two pounds went nowhere when you had a mobile to run. Shit, his text messages alone cost half of that! So he supplemented his income by finding lost golf balls and selling them to the professional at the golf club, who gave him fifty pence each for them, and who in turn sold them on for a pound each to the Sunnymere members for use as practice balls.

Jason, not being a member of the golf club, wasn't allowed to search for balls on the golf course itself, but golf balls have a habit of flying over boundary walls and

59

depositing themselves in adjacent fields and woods, a useful quality for anyone seeking a constant supply of used golf balls, and it was these locations that provided Jason with his harvest.

Not long after he had embarked upon his career in the golf ball recycling industry Jason discovered that Tobin was re-selling the balls on for an additional fifty pence, and shortly after that the boy, surely an entrepreneur of the future, hit upon the idea of cutting out the middle man and selling his golf balls direct to the golfers. This brought him twice the revenue it previously had, for the same effort, which seemed to Jason to be too good to be true. It was. For it wasn't long before he inadvertently tried to sell a golfer one of his own marked golf balls back (Tobin could never have made such a mistake), much to the golfer's annoyance. Not too long ago Jason would have received a clout round the ear-hole for his pains, but that option is unfortunately no longer available to adults in the enlightened times of the twenty first century, unless they fancy spending some poor quality time in a police station lock-up before being hauled in front of the magistrates, so in retribution the irate golfer had contented himself with treading on Jason's foot with his spiked shoe, an action which he claimed was a complete accident and for which he was very sorry. Jason, ending up with half a dozen small holes through the top of his new designer trainers, through his sock, and in his foot, would have preferred a clout round the ear-hole every time.

On some days golf ball pickings weren't as good as they were on others, and if one such day coincided with a time when Jason was in dire need of a top-up card for his mobile or the latest Lily Allen CD a more positive ball-finding method had to be adopted. This method took the form of finding lost golf balls within the precincts of the golf course, and when really desperate measures were called for, say when he was in dire need of a top-up card for his mobile *and* Lily Allen's latest CD, finding lost balls on the golf course before they were actually lost. One such day was Captain's Day.

—◦◦◦—

Having driven off, Armitage and Stock were walking up the fairway together, Grover lagging a few yards or so behind having stopped to tie his shoelace.

"Do you think size matters, Gerard?" said Armitage to his companion, conversationally.

"Size?"

"Yes. Do you think it matters?"

Stock pretended to give the matter some thought. "Yes," he said after a moment or two. "Most definitely."

It wasn't the answer Armitage had been seeking. Disappointment wreathed his face. "Really?"

"Oh absolutely," confirmed Stock. "Yes, if you don't use size your wallpaper can drop off."

Armitage's brow wrinkled in puzzlement. "What?" Then he realised Stock had misunderstood his question. "No. No, not that size. The size of your todger. The size of your penis. Do you think it matters, you know, to a woman?"

Catching up with them Grover had caught the tail end of the conversation. "Is he going on about dicks again, Gerard?" he asked of Stock.

"Do bears shit on the Pope?"

Grover turned his attention to Armitage. "What's the matter Trevor, have you got a little one or something?"

"You wouldn't like it in your eye," said Armitage.

—⚹—

Up ahead Arbuthnott, Bagley and Chapman were playing the sixth. Arbuthnott, after the very promising start to his round, had let things slip a little over the last two holes, taking a bogey five at the fourth and a double-bogey five at the par three fifth, but even allowing for that slight double hiccup he was still two shots under the card after taking his stroke allowance into consideration. Now things started to get back on track as his seven iron approach shot hit the top of one of the greenside bunkers before fortuitously being thrown onto the green and coming to rest no more than twenty feet from the flag.

"Wham!" Arbuthnott shouted in delight. "Yet *another* birdie opportunity."

"Jammy bugger," said Chapman.

"This is better than sex," said Arbuthnott, ignoring Chapman's jibe.

Bagley looked at Arbuthnott as though his playing partner was quite mad. "Who are you having sex with?"

"What?"

"Well if making a birdie was better than the sex I was getting I'd be looking around for somebody else to have it with."

"There's nothing wrong with the sex I'm getting," said Arbuthnott, a little piqued. "It's probably every bit as good as the sex you're getting. If not better. Your problem, Baggers, is that you don't make enough birdies to compare the relative methods of having sex and making a birdie."

"And your problem, Arby, is that you're doing far too much standing about bragging about how good you are and not enough getting on with the bloody game," said Chapman, who himself was still faring nothing like so well as Arbuthnott, and making no attempt to hide the disappointment which accompanied that unhappy state of affairs. "You know how my game suffers if I'm forced to play slowly," he went on grumpily. "Someone less charitable than me might think you were playing slowly deliberately."

Whilst not wishing to get into an argument in case it should spoil his own game Arbuthnott felt that he couldn't let this slur on his character pass unchallenged. "Playing slowly? Me? How can I be playing slowly? Up to now you've taken about twice as many shots as I have, so even if I were taking twice as long to play them, which I'm not, I'd still only be taking as long to play the game as you are."

Chapman had no answer to Arbuthnott's logic, which although he didn't care for, couldn't fault. It didn't stop him replying however. "Oh stop crowing," he said, and turned his back on Arbuthnott, bringing an end to the altercation.

—⚬—

On the first tee Mr Captain hoped against hope that he had seen the last of the naked youth. A naked youth running around the golf was the very last thing he wanted. Good Lord, what if the reprobate chose to put in another appearance when the Lord Mayor was in attendance! That would be the end, an unmitigated disaster, it didn't even bear thinking about.

Immediately following the incident, and after he had recovered from the shock, Mr Captain had considered calling in the police to track down and apprehend the naked trespasser. However he didn't want the police running around the golf course spoiling his Captain's Day no more than he wanted unclothed youths running around spoiling it, so dismissed the idea from his mind no sooner than it had entered it. He had enough to worry about as it was, with the weather.

For about the tenth time since Ifield had issued his gloomy forecast he checked the sky for any alteration in its condition. The weather seemed to be holding up, no sign of any change yet. But Ifield had been quite adamant about it, and the English weather can change so quickly, so it might only be a matter of time. He made the decision not to look at the sky again as it was only making him feel depressed, but on returning his gaze to eye level he saw something else that immediately gave him as much concern as the weather, in the shape of his wife Millicent, who was now hurrying towards him. What on earth was she doing here at this time? She wasn't due to arrive until shortly before the first of the golfers were due to call in at the beer tent so obviously something must have cropped up, some snag or other. He just hoped it wasn't serious. But as Millicent drew closer to him he could see from the tight-lipped expression on her face that it was very serious, and when she joined him she quickly confirmed his fears. "I'm afraid I have some rather bad news for you, Henry," she said, placing a supportive hand on his forearm, bonding them together, as was her habit whenever the couple faced difficulties.

His eyes widened in apprehension. "It's not going to spoil my day is it Millicent?"

"Not necessarily," said Millicent, giving him cause for hope and cause for concern in equal measure. "It's concerning the band for the dance this evening."

"The Syncopation Four?"

"I'm afraid they can't come."

"Can't come?" This was terrible. A disaster. What on earth had Millicent meant with her 'not necessarily', this sounded to him like a cast iron copper-bottomed certainty to spoil his day. No band, no dance, simple as that. "What do you mean they can't come?"

"They rang a half hour ago to say they'd double-booked by mistake."

"Double-booked?" The darkness that had descended upon Mr Captain lifted as he immediately saw a solution to the problem. "Then the Syncopation Four must simply tell whoever else they are double-booked with that they can't keep to the arrangement due to circumstances beyond their control, and honour their agreement with us."

"That is what I told them. My exact words. But they said the other party had booked first so they felt duty bound to give them precedence."

Mr Captain bristled. "What? And what do they think we are supposed to do? This is intolerable, Millicent, quite intolerable."

Millicent applied a little comforting pressure to her husband's arm. "Calm down, Henry. All is not lost. We'll get through this. Together. The Hamiltons."

The Fridlingtons liked to compare the closeness of their relationship to that of the marriage of ex-Member of Parliament Neil Hamilton and his wife Christine, both Henry and Millicent firmly believing that Neil Hamilton was totally innocent of the charges that brought about his downfall. Indeed it wouldn't be an exaggeration to say that the Hamiltons were their idols, (Millicent looked not unlike Christine which may have coloured their judgement somewhat), so much so that if someone were to tell the Fridlingtons that they reminded them of the Hamiltons they would have taken it not as the insult for which it had probably been intended, but as the highest compliment it was possible to pay them.

"The Hamiltons!" echoed Mr Captain, as if proposing a toast of thanks to the disgraced politician and his graceless wife.

"However," Millicent went on, "after I had received the bad news I wasted no time in contacting the agency through which we booked them to see if they had another band free for this evening. But they said they hadn't, at such short notice. However they did put me in touch with another agency who they said might be able to help."

"And could they?" said Mr Captain eagerly, hoping against hope.

"They had a choice of two. 'Lord Nose and the Bogies' was one."

"Oh I don't like the sound of them."

"Neither did I. The other choice was a disco, 'Daddy Rhythm'."

Mr Captain pulled a face. "I don't like the sound of him either. I don't like the sound of discos, full stop."

"Nor me Henry, as you know. But on questioning the agent further I was told that the sort of performance put on by Lord Nose and the Bogies could be regarded by some as a bit near the knuckle, so..."

"...you opted for Daddy Rhythm?"

"The lesser of two evils, I thought. Anyway he'll be here shortly."

"At this early hour?"

"Apparently he's busy this afternoon so he'll need to set up his equipment this morning. Nothing for you to worry about, I'll keep an eye open for him and spell things out to him as regards just what is and is not acceptable at a golf club dinner dance. We certainly don't want him playing the sort of rubbish disc-jockeys usually play."

"Indeed we do not, Millicent. Especially when we will be entertaining the Lord Mayor."

"My thoughts entirely. Leave it with me Henry, I'll put this Daddy Rhythm person on the straight and narrow and ensure that he doesn't stray off it."

—⚹—

Hanson wasn't such a bad bloke to play with, mused Galloway, as the two of them walked side by side up the fifth fairway. He didn't, like so many playing partners, put you off when you were putting by standing in your

65

eye-line, and he was always generous with his praise when you made a good shot or holed a tricky putt. If only he didn't go on about his multitude of illnesses all the time!

Galloway had played quite often with Hanson, and, like Hanson's state of health, it never got any better. During their round Hanson would go through all his illnesses from A to Z. Galloway wasn't sure if there were any illnesses beginning with Z but if there were he was sure Hanson would be suffering from them. Hanson would always start to trawl through his litany of ailments very early in the round, thus ensuring he had adequate time to fit them all in. He would begin with his head and work down, using his body as a sort of index to make sure he didn't forget anything.

By the time they had reached the fifth fairway Galloway had been advised on the latest state of Hanson's illnesses up to, or perhaps down to, his rheumatoid arthritis-ridden knee. His head was no better. Worse if anything. He was still having these bangs that had started about two years ago. They were just like simultaneous flashes of lightning and claps of thunder. He wouldn't wish them on his worst enemy. He was getting them more frequently now, at least once a week, for about two days' duration, then they would go, just as quickly as they'd arrived. He had seen his doctor about them, and several consultant neurologists, one of whom was a knight of the realm. None of whom had known what the hell they were talking about. He might as well have gone to a vet.

His neck was no better. It never would be. It was absolutely shot. Completely riddled with arthritis. By now he couldn't turn his head more than twenty degrees to the right, and he didn't like to turn it even that far as the last time he'd done so it had triggered off the sudden bangs in his head again.

His frozen shoulder was a bit better but that was a sure sign it was going to get worse if the last time it had started to feel a bit better was anything to go by.

His chest pains, caused by his hiatus hernia, were thankfully no worse, but they were bad enough. The same couldn't be said for his back, which was a *lot* worse. Since the last time he'd played with Galloway he'd had another X-ray and the doctor had told him they couldn't find anything wrong with him and had shown him the X-ray, which confirmed the doctor's diagnosis, but it must have been somebody else's X-ray, there must have been a mix-up or something, it stood to reason, otherwise why was his back still killing him?

His anal pain was a pain in the arse, if Galloway would pardon the expression; worse than it had ever been and getting even worse by the minute. He had tried just about everything, you name it he'd tried it. Conventional medicine, acupuncture, homeopathy, hypnotherapy, aromatherapy, even therapy without a prefix, all to no avail. It felt just like somebody was shoving a cricket stump up his behind. It was only the blunt end of a cricket stump as yet, but he was sure it was only a matter of time before it developed into the pointed end, along with a couple of bails for good measure. He had even tried, in absolute desperation, going to a faith healer, a travelling evangelist. At the meeting the faith healer had laid hands on a man's lips and apparently cured his long-standing speech impediment, then he'd laid hands on a woman's gammy leg with the same result, but he had done nothing at all for Hanson's bottom when he had laid hands on it. However Hanson had noted that the faith healer hadn't spent anything like so much time with his hands on his bottom as he had on the other two's lips and leg, which no doubt had something to do with it. He would have demanded his money back but it was free, so he had contented himself with putting nothing in the collection box and taking a pound coin out as compensation for having had his time wasted.

His prostate trouble was just about holding its own and he still couldn't get a full erection. He'd had pills for both but neither had worked, although the pill he'd taken for his erection problem had eased his prostate trouble a little whilst doing absolutely nothing for him in the tumescence department.

His arthritic knee was definitely worse. It was now twice as big as his other knee, which itself was twice as big as it should be, on account of it having water on it.

Galloway had twice tried to steer the conversation on to another subject, but to no avail. He would have had more chance trying to stop a cattle stampede with a water pistol. When Hanson had stopped to draw breath - which incidentally he was becoming much shorter of these days whenever he walked up hills, the doctor didn't know why but then he didn't know anything – Galloway had remarked, "I believe the weather's going to turn colder tomorrow." Hanson had immediately replied with, "It won't be as cold as my foot. It's like ice my foot. Hardening of the arteries you see. Not a thing to be done for it," he added, taking a deep drag on his cigarette and setting his dry cough off again.

Galloway hadn't bothered to make any further attempts to stem the flow, satisfied that having inadvertently drawn Hanson's attention to his cold foot he had caused him to miss out his sore shins and fallen arches. Hanson now moved on to the verruca on his heel, no better, and then to the last of his maladies, his hammer-toe, which was now worse since the last time they'd spoken due to it having developed a painful corn on it. He had seen a chiropodist last week and she had never seen anything like it in her life, had never set eyes on such a nasty looking corn and hoped never to set eyes on another, it was far beyond her scope, he would need an operation, but there was a four year waiting list so he'd just have to go on suffering.

At least I won't have to go on suffering, thought Galloway, as he breathed a sigh of relief on the completion of the tour of Hanson's sick body, having had more than enough of his ailments. Pleased that he would now be able to concentrate on his golf Galloway congratulated himself that he'd got off relatively lightly this time as the last time they'd played together they'd reached the ninth green before Hanson had completed his catalogue of illnesses.

They continued walking down the fairway towards their golf balls.

"And the wife is just as bad," said Hanson. "She has this…."

H Jackman (8)
P Keaney (12)
B Littler (17)

Waiting to tee off at the first, Harry Jackman, Peter Keaney and Bernard Littler were all standing deep in thought. Mr Captain, observing this from a few yards away, was about to ask them if he could help them with whatever problem they appeared to be wrestling with when suddenly Jackman shouted out the single word "Fluffing!"

Keaney and Littler considered Jackman's proclamation for a moment or two, but without any great enthusiasm. Littler wasn't keen all. It was better than nothing he supposed, but it wasn't the one. Keaney felt much the same way. "Not bad," he said, "But I'm sure we can do better."

The three gave the matter further thought and Mr Captain was again about to break in on their musings to see if he could be of assistance when Keaney, suddenly inspired, cried out "Mucky Nell!"

Jackman and Littler were immediately impressed. This was more like it.

"Oh yes," congratulated the former, "Yes, I like that. I like that a lot."

"Me too," said Littler. "It sounds just the ticket."

Jackman turned to Mr Captain and called, "What say you, Mr Captain?"

"What's that, Harry?" said Mr Captain, closing in on them.

Jackman explained. "Now that we aren't allowed to swear we're trying to find a suitable alternative for when we feel the need to say effing hell. Peter has suggested 'Mucky Nell'."

"We've already got an alternative for the C-word," Littler added.

"Kunt," said Keaney. "Spelt with a 'K'. An old Norse word we're told. It means a young cat, apparently. It will need your approval, of course."

"Well it won't be getting it," snapped Mr Captain, and made a mental note to add the K-word to the list of other words that were banned.

"But what do you think to Mucky Nell as an alternative to effing hell?" Jackman persisted.

Mr Captain treated the threesome to a withering glare. "What I think is that the three of you would be far better employed concentrating your minds on not using the F-word or the C-word, thus safeguarding your position as members of this golf club, rather than wasting your time trying to find alternatives for them," he barked, sententiously. "One man has already booked himself an appointment with the General Committee this morning."

"For swearing?" asked Little.

"For swearing," affirmed Mr Captain.

"Who was it?" said Jackman.

"George Fidler."

"Mucky Nell!" said Keaney.

—⁂—

The best place to thieve golf balls, Jason had found, was about halfway down the long par five third, where rich pickings were always to be had. This was because the area where the balls came to rest was in a hollow in the fairway, which gathered them in, and which was obscured from the tee some two hundred and fifty yards distant by a large hillock. Thus after all the tee shots had been played it gave a ball thief ample time to climb over the boundary wall, purloin one of the balls, and be safe back over the other side of the wall before the golfers came into view. Not wishing to cook the goose that laid the golden eggs, Jason only ever took one of the balls, as to take more might lead the golfers into suspecting something was amiss, whereas one lost ball wouldn't draw any suspicion, a single golfer losing his ball being nearer the norm at Sunnymere rather than something out of the ordinary. And why take the risk? Golfers in groups of three and four were like buses, there'd be another one along in a few minutes, and he'd be able to steal one of their balls too to add to his booty.

One such ball now skipped down the hill and came to rest in the hollow, joining the two that were already there. Jason wasted no time about it, nipped over the wall, ran quickly onto the fairway, pocketed the nearest of the balls, and was back behind the wall and into hiding in the time you can say Dunlop 65, which is what the ball happened to be.

—⁂—

Tobin wasn't at all happy about the fact that Grover's Nike sweater had stretched; or titted, as Grover had so graphically described its condition. Something was definitely wrong. In the professional's experience Nike sweaters had never stretched before and he must have sold hundreds of them in the seven years he'd been dealing with the company, although, as far as he knew, none of the men's sweaters he had sold thus far had ever been subjected to having a pair of ladies' breasts in them for an hour or two. But even bearing that in mind it shouldn't have happened; this was a quality garment you were talking about here, surely it should have reverted back to its original shape once the offending breasts had been removed? Tobin decided the only thing for it was to conduct an experiment in order to find out for certain. Darren was the chosen guinea pig. "Put this on, Darren," he said to his assistant, handing him a Nike sweater, "I want to try something out."

Unquestioningly, for you do not question the motives of a man who is smart enough to know the golf kit requirements of every member of the club, Darren slipped the sweater over his head.

Tobin looked around for something that might fill in as breasts. Golf balls? No, too small. Golf shoes? Too big. And the wrong shape, unless you were trying to duplicate the pendulous appendages of Mrs Rattray. Golf club head covers? They would do perhaps, if stuffed with something to make them firm. He took a few pairs of socks from a shelf and stuffed a couple of pairs into each of the two woollen head covers, then put the covers up Darren's sweater in the approximate position of a pair of breasts.

Darren looked down at his newly-acquired falsies. "Awesome."

"Leave them there for an hour or two, we'll see if they stretch the sweater any," said Tobin. However as he stepped back to inspect his handiwork he observed that the breasts weren't quite right, the right one being a bit higher than the left and the left one a touch too far left, so he took one in each hand and commenced to jiggle them around to get them in the right position.

And was thus indirectly responsible for contributing hugely to the spoiling of Mr Captain's Day.

—⚬—

The quick walk from her home to the golf club had made Millicent's throat dry – she hoped it wasn't one of her summer colds coming on – and she had decided on her way to the clubhouse to await the arrival of Daddy Rhythm that she would call in at the pro's shop for a tube of those eucalyptus lozenges he sold. She would have bought something for her throat elsewhere had it been convenient, as she didn't at all care for Tobin. She didn't care for tradesmen in general, considering them a necessary evil, but she especially didn't like avaricious charlatans like Sunnymere's professional.

In consequence of this she patronised his shop only when absolutely necessary, and even then only for articles she couldn't readily obtain elsewhere, such as golf clubs and balls. The clothes she golfed in were purchased from Debenhams in Derby, where one could guarantee the quality, and whose sales assistants didn't try to sell you the entire contents of the shop every time you set foot in it.

In fact Millicent, aided and abetted by Mr Captain, planned to get rid of Tobin at the earliest possible convenience. It was just a matter of how and when, and of the right opportunity presenting itself.

It had dawned on Millicent some time ago that Tobin was relieving the members of Sunnymere of a great deal of their money. She didn't know how much exactly but she suspected it to be a very substantial amount. The man drove a this year's registration Mercedes SL for goodness sake and you didn't buy those with tram tickets. An educated guess at Tobin's annual turnover, arrived at by a combination of spending long periods watching people enter his shop and observing what they came out with, and simply by asking golfing friends what they had bought from Tobin on the pretext of comparing prices, put the figure in the region of two hundred and fifty thousand pounds a year. Profits, so far as she was able to discern, would be at least a hundred thousand pounds. Why should that hundred thousand pounds go to Tobin, she had asked herself? Why did it take the services of a professional golfer to sell sweaters and shirts and trousers and such? Anyone could do that. Get rid of Tobin and the hundred thousand pounds profit, less the government minimum wages you would have to pay for a couple of young shop assistants to run the shop, would benefit the club. Especially the ladies' section, whose locker room was in dire need of a new carpet and pretty curtains, if not a complete make-over including a more extensive and luxurious powder room and a Jacuzzi. But with the best part of a hundred thousand pounds extra income coming into the club every year plans could be made for even more than those absolute necessities.

—⁂—

Whilst he was still jiggling Darren's artificial breasts around, something suddenly dawned on Tobin. The thought of it caused his jaw to drop in surprise. "She hasn't got any tits!" he blurted out.

"What?" said Darren.

"Grover's wife! She hasn't got any tits!" He quoted from memory, "Grover, Betty. Nike Sweaters, bust 32, A Cup. Betty Grover hasn't got any tits, Darren!"

"I beg your pardon!" came an outraged voice from behind him.

Tobin wheeled round. Standing there was Millicent Fridlington, her body quivering with indignation, her face absolutely livid.

His mind fully occupied with getting Darren's artificial breasts positioned correctly, followed immediately by the realisation that Betty Grover had no breasts to speak of and therefore couldn't have done to Grover's sweater what Grover had alleged they had, Tobin had failed to notice Millicent enter the shop. When he did, courtesy of Millicent's outburst, he knew immediately that he was in trouble. Big time. If it had been a male member whom he had just informed that Betty Grover had no tits he might have got away with it, and even some of the lady members might not have been too concerned, especially the ones who did have tits, indeed they might even have been pleased; but it wasn't a male member, it was that bloody dragon Millicent Fridlington, the wife of Mr Captain!

"S...Sorry, Mrs Fridlington," Tobin stammered. "I didn't see you there."

"I would have thought that was entirely obvious," Millicent stormed.

"Or I would never have said it."

"Oh, so if I hadn't been here it wouldn't have stopped you saying that horrible thing about poor Mrs Grover?"

"Wh...what?"

"Or fondling that young boy in that disgusting manner, like some perverted paedophile?"

By this time Tobin was floundering like a freshly caught mackerel in the bottom of a fishing boat. "Wh...what?" he stammered. "No. I mean...well it just slipped out, Mrs Fridlington, I didn't mean anything by it. Of course Mrs Grover has got tits...breasts.... bosoms. Not that I go around looking at women's..... And I wasn't fondling Darren, I was just..."

Millicent interrupted him, raising her hand like a particularly officious traffic policeman. "You can save your ridiculous excuses for my husband. Although I doubt very much it will do you any good." With that she turned on her heel and walked out of the shop, a far happier woman than when she had walked in. The opportunity to get rid of Tobin had presented itself. It would be taken, and without delay.

—⁓—

Garland, Harris and Ifield reached the top of the hill at the third and started the descent that led to the hollow in the fairway, some hundred or so yards away. All three had hit decent tee shots and fully expected to find their balls on the fairway, although Garland's shot had been a little farther left than he had intended, and with the bit of accidental slice he usually put on the ball he thought he might just have ended up in the fairway bunker placed there for that very purpose. On the walk to their balls Ifield and Harris conjectured on this likelihood. "I wonder if the gentleman is in the bunker," conjectured Ifield, "or if the bastard is on the fairway?"

In fact, when they arrived in the hollow, Garland was neither.

"That's odd," said Garland. "I didn't think I was all that far off line."

"Must have got a bad kick," said, Harris. "Threw the ball into the rough probably."

The three of them searched around in the long grass between the fairway and the boundary wall but without success, except that Ifield found a ball he had lost there the last time he played, which he said was 'just his bloody luck', and the five minutes allowed by the rules for searching for a lost ball were almost up and the frustrated Garland was about to set off on 'The Green Mile', the long and lonely walk back to the tee to play another ball, when Jason coughed.

It wasn't a very loud cough, not much more than a clearing of the throat, but it was loud enough to attract Garland's attention.

Making as little noise as possible Garland crept over to the wall and peered over the other side. His luck was in. Had he been a few yards farther on or back Jason would have seen him and escaped, but the boy was directly in front of him, and before he could make a run for it Garland grabbed him by the hair.

"What have we here then?" he said, in triumph.

"Ow, you're hurting me!" protested Jason, squirming and trying to unclamp Garland's hand from his hair. "Let me go, you're sodding hurting me!"

"Shut it you little toerag," said Garland, tightening his grip on Jason's locks. He dragged him bodily over the wall, took him by the scruff of the neck and frog-marched him over to the fairway where Harris and Ifield were waiting with interest. "The little sod's pinched my ball," he explained to them.

"I haven't and you can't prove it," said Jason.

Garfield grabbed him by the shoulders and turned him round. "Empty your pockets!"

"I'm going to report you for child abuse. You're not allowed to do things like that nowadays, you're not even allowed to touch me."

"Shut your ugly little cakehole and empty your pockets!"

"No, and you can't make me," said Jason, defiantly, jutting out his bottom lip.

Garland shook him violently. "I said empty your pockets you little twat before I empty them for you!"

There was no way Jason was going to empty his pockets, his mobile phone was in there for a start, and he certainly didn't want the man getting hold of that, adults could be mean, and this one looked very mean and he might damage it just for spite or even pinch it. He put his hand in his right hand trousers pocket and pulled out the golf ball. Garland snatched it off him and identified it as his own. "Just as I suspected." He glared at Jason. "This is mine. You've just nicked it off the fairway."

"I thought it was lost."

"You'll wish you were lost when I've finished with you, you horrible little turd."

"What are you going to do with him, Mr Vice?" asked Harris.

Garland thought for a moment. "Have either of you got any rope on you?"

"Christ you're not going to hang him are you?" said Ifield, not completely convinced he was speaking only in jest. "That's a bit extreme, isn't it?"

"Don't tempt me, Justin. No, I'm going to tie him to my trolley until we get round to the ninth if I can find anything to tie him with, then turn the little bleeder in."

"I've got a spare pair of shoelaces in my bag," offered Harris.

"They'll do."

—⚬⚬⚬—

Mrs Quayle, Mrs Rattray and Mrs Salinas were by now nearing the thirteenth green.

"Eight ounces of cheese," said Mrs Salinas. "Two ounces of…"

Mrs Quayle, a stickler where the accuracy of recipes was concerned, butted in. "What sort of cheese?"

"Sorry Miriam, I forget exactly the cheese that Delia stipulated."

"Blast."

"It will need to be a mild cheese, though. Nothing too overpowering. Certainly not parmesan or a blue cheese. I used Wensleydale."

"Oh Harold and I went there a few weeks back, Wensleydale," said Mrs Rattray.

"Beautiful, isn't it," said Mrs Quayle.

"Absolutely lovely," said Mrs Salinas.

—⚬⚬⚬—

Due no doubt to being distracted by the sight of Carter being chased by the teenager with the enviable penis it wasn't until he was approaching the second green that Armitage realised he hadn't eaten the space cake.

Armitage, although he had reached his thirty fifth year some months ago, had not until the previous week, and unlike the vast majority of people of his age, ever experimented with drugs. It wasn't that he had anything against drugs - he didn't mind other people taking them, if that's what turned them on that was their affair, let them get on with it and good luck to them - it was just that he had never felt the need of them. And this state of affairs would probably have remained for evermore had he not visited his brother Brian in Nottingham the week previously.

During the visit Brian had asked him if he had ever had a space cake. Armitage hadn't even known what a space cake was and if he'd had to hazard a guess would have said it was part of the rations carried by astronauts, or maybe some sort of confectionary with a space in the middle of it like a doughnut, but on being informed by Brian that it was a chocolate brownie fortified with cannabis Armitage had said that no he hadn't, nor did he want to have one thank you very much. Brian had said that was the way he himself had felt about space cakes until he'd been persuaded into trying one by a friend, and that following on from it, and whilst under the influence of it, he had played the best game of snooker in his life. He had put it down to the relaxing influence of the cannabis freeing up his cue action to such an extent that it had had the effect of making even quite a difficult pot seem easy. "The pot made it easier to pot," he had remarked at the time.

Armitage, a keen snooker player himself when not on the golf course, but about as skilled a practitioner of the sport as he was at golf, which was somewhere between distinctly average and not very good at all, wondered if a space cake might do the same for him. There was only one way to find out.

When he returned home the following day, armed with one of the half dozen space cakes generously donated by Brian, he made the local snooker club his first port of call. After eating the space cake and giving it half-an-hour to get fully into his system, as directed by Brian, he then played a frame of snooker. The result was nothing short of miraculous. All his senses were now enhanced, everything was much bigger and brighter. He felt so light; not light-headed – heavier-headed if anything – but light on his feet, as though walking on air. In his hand the cue didn't feel more like a broom handle than a snooker cue, as it usually did, but like a magician's wand, and like a magician's wand it soon began to weave its magic. He couldn't credit just how much the relaxing influence of the space cake had improved his game. The impossible shots became merely difficult, the difficult shots considerably easier, and the easier shots a walk in the park. His previous highest-ever break, compiled over twenty two painstaking minutes, five of which had been spent in the lavatory where he'd had to go to relieve himself due to the excitement of getting past twenty for the first time, had been thirty one, and was only that high because he'd fluked a red off three cushions when he was on fifteen. He passed that humble score in two minutes flat. He didn't achieve his first-ever fifty break, but only because he got a little too cocky and tried to pot an almost impossible pink off two cushions, left-handed, when the brown or blue would have been much a much easier option.

A cautious man by nature, Armitage wondered if perhaps the whole thing was a coincidence, and that he might have performed just as well even if he hadn't had the space cake, that it had perhaps acted as a placebo, so the following day he went back to the snooker club and played a frame without having the advantage of a space cake inside him. He was absolutely terrible; the wand had disappeared, the broom handle back in place. However a space cake soon put that right, as after re-racking the balls and playing another frame he found that he was as good as he was the day before, better in fact, as on this occasion he cut out the fancy stuff and made a break of seventy eight. There was no doubt about it then, a space cake, simply by relaxing you and heightening your senses, did wonders for your snooker.

It wasn't long before Armitage got to wondering if what held good for snooker might also hold good for golf, which was why he was now approaching the second green having just realised he'd forgotten to eat one of the space cakes before setting out on his round. He now reached into the ball pocket of his bag, in which he had stowed a couple of the cannabis-loaded sweetmeats, took one out and quickly ate it. Suitably charged he now looked forward to breaking the course record.

—⁓—

"Wasn't it Macbeth?" said Mrs Quayle?

"Hamlet, I think," said Mrs Salinas.

"It was certainly one of the tragedies. I'm sure it was Macbeth."

"No, it was *Wharfedale*," said Mrs Rattray, rejoining the others from the private world in which she had been dwelling for the last minute or so.

Mrs Quayle and Mrs Salinas looked at her in surprise. "What was?" asked Mrs Quayle.

"Where Harold and I went the other weekend. It wasn't Wensleydale, it was Wharfedale."

"Oh that's very nice too," enthused Mrs Salinas. "And less sheep." She thought for a moment before continuing, "Of course they don't have the cheese there. If you want beauty *and* cheese you have to go to Wensleydale."

"Or Marks and Spencers," said Mrs Quayle.

"Or Marks and Spencers," agreed Mrs Rattray.

S Cuddington (24)
G Treforest (24)
R Jones-Jones (24)

The next three gentlemen to grace the first tee with their presence at Sunnymere that day were Sylvester Cuddington, Ged Treforest, and Rhys Jones-Jones. Like many club golfers throughout England's green and pleasant land, and probably every other land where golf is played, green, pleasant or otherwise, the three friends invariably played together in club competitions. What was different about Cuddington, Treforest and Jones-Jones however was that in addition to sharing each other's company they also shared afflictions, although not the same one - Cuddington was a hunchback, Treforest had a club foot, whilst Jones-Jones, perhaps appropriately in view of his surname, had a stutter - and it was these physical handicaps, along with their respective long golf handicaps, that had drawn and bonded them together. Gallows humour is by no means a stranger to golf clubs and collectively the three were known throughout the club as 'Casualty'.

There is no other man in the whole wide world who is as optimistic as a golfer standing on the first tee. As he is about to set forth on another round of golf he knows for sure that he is going to play well. It doesn't matter that the last time he took to the greensward he played like a drain, nor the time before he would have been hard-pressed to hit a cow's behind with a banjo, never mind a distant green with a three iron; a man fancying his chances of getting hand relief in a dodgy massage parlour could not be more optimistic of success than a golfer stood on the first tee.

There are seldom grounds for such optimism. But then why should there be? For there can be no earthly reason for it. Why should a swing which has consistently got its owner into more trouble than the Americans got themselves into in Vietnam suddenly start working properly? Why should a swing that in the past has always contrived to dispatch a golf ball in any direction but the correct one, and about half the intended distance, suddenly transform itself into something that could propel a golf ball forward, arrow straight, and the correct distance? Why should the player's skill with a sand wedge suddenly improve when every time he had previously called upon the services of that club to get him out of trouble it had succeeded only in getting him into even more trouble by removing from the bunker enough sand to build a dozen moderately-sized sandcastles, whilst at the same time contriving to leave the ball in the bunker, and in a much worse lie? And why should a putting stroke that for the last twenty years had managed to ensure that the ball consistently missed the hole with unerring certainty suddenly start causing the ball to find the centre of the hole?

Nevertheless the golfer will always remain optimistic. Never mind that the last time he played he posted his worst score ever. Never mind that on arriving home he had kicked the dog and thrown his clubs into the garage and vowed never to play golf again as long as he drew breath. Never mind that he had told his wife that if he ever so much as mentioned the word golf again, let alone play it, he would buy her a complete new wardrobe. Since then the penny will have dropped. He will have finally realised at long last that for all the years he has been playing his grip has been wrong; or that he has been leaning too far forward in his stance, or not far enough; or that he has been standing too near to the ball, or too far away from it; or he has had the ball too far back in his stance, or too far forward. Or his knees have been bent too much or not bent enough. Or his feet have been too far apart, or too near to each other. Now, having made the necessary adjustment, things would be hunky dory.

Or perhaps the problem might not have been physical, but mental. The golfer may have realised he was too tense and uptight, so had invested in a relaxation tape and had benefited from its soothing words of wisdom. Now, fully relaxed and downtight, he would finally be able to do himself justice. Or he may have realised he was *too* relaxed, and to counteract this had presented himself on the first tee after first having psyched himself up for the previous six hours by standing naked in a barrelful of crabs.

Or he may have had a lesson from the professional. As was the case with Sylvester Cuddington.

"Oh by the way," said that very golfer to his companions as he teed up his ball, "I've had a lesson since we last played."

"I'd b-better g-go for my t-tin hat," said Jones-Jones.

Treforest too was well aware of the doubtful benefits of a golf lesson. "Get one for me while you're at it, Taff; I'll need one if he hits the ball anything like he did the last time he had a lesson."

"No need for tin hats, Ged," said Cuddington, oozing confidence, "Or any other protection for that matter. I'm very straight now, swinging like an Open winner, the pro really sorted out me out."

"Tobin?" said Treforest in disbelief. "It would take him all his time to sort out an empty cupboard."

Jones-Jones was quick to agree, though not as quick in conveying his agreement, due to his stutter. "I should s-say s-so. He's r-rubbish, that T-Tobin. He's m-more interested in s-selling you a new s-sweater than t-teaching you how to play golf p-properly."

Cuddington however, far from defending Tobin, shared his playing partner's opinion of the Sunnymere professional. "I didn't go to Tobin," he said. "Complete waste of money. No, I went to that new bloke they've got at the Municipal. He talked a lot of sense."

"What did he have to say?" asked Treforest, hopeful that the teachings of the professional at the nearby municipal golf course might improve his own game, where others had failed.

"First he told me it was absolutely pointless him trying to teach me how to swing a golf club correctly," said Cuddington.

"Because of your hump?" said Treforest.

Cuddington didn't mind people referring to his hump no more than Treforest and Jones-Jones minded people bringing up their afflictions in conversation. All had been born with their burdens and were by now quite comfortable with them, although Cuddington didn't much care for being called Quasimodo, which he had been on several occasions, once, appropriately if somewhat insensitively, outside Notre Dame Cathedral; but never by a golfer.

"No he said it was my age," continued Cuddington. "He said that over the years I'd picked up too many bad habits which I'd never get rid of now no matter how hard I tried. He said I would be far better off living with my bad habits and adapting to them, and that as long as I remembered to make the same mistakes with my downswing as I'd made with my backswing I wouldn't go far wrong."

"M-make the same mistakes with your d-downswing as you d-do with your b-backswing?"

"Make as many mistakes coming down as you did going up, was the way he put it," affirmed Cuddington. "And not even necessarily in the same order. And it works too. He had me hitting the ball better than I've ever hit it in my life. I hit one drive two hundred and fifty yards"

Jones-Jones was impressed. "T-two hundred and f-fifty yards? I d-don't g-go that f-far on my h-holidays."

Watching them, Mr Captain, showing a little concern, now called over to them. "You'd better get a move on, gentlemen," he said, pointing at his watch, "You'll be holding up the next group if you're not careful."

"Right away, Mr Captain," said Cuddington, and putting his newly acquired skill to good use proceeded to hit a booming drive that split the fairway.

Jones-Jones and Treforest watched the ball disappear into the distance and come to rest some two hundred and thirty yards away. Jones-Jones was even more impressed now he had witnessed Cuddington's words transformed into reality. "I m-might have a g-go at that myself," he said. "How about you, G-Ged?"

"Does the Pope shit on Catholics?" said Treforest.

—◊◊◊—

Due to her having had to report Tobin's unseemly but fortuitous behaviour to her husband without delay, the disc-jockey was already setting up his equipment when Millicent swept into the golf club's function room. She hadn't expected to like what she saw and Daddy Rhythm's appearance did nothing to belie her expectations, fat forty-year-olds with purple Mohican haircuts and green lipstick being far from her favourite example of *Homo sapiens*. At least the yob wasn't wearing earrings, Millicent noted, thankfully. "I am the wife of Mr Captain," she said to him imperiously, losing no time in making her exalted position in the hierarchy of the golf club clear to Daddy Rhythm, should he be under the illusion that he was dealing with the hired help.

Daddy Rhythm, taking his cue from Millicent, thinking perhaps that it was the usual form of address in golfing circles said, "I am the husband of Mrs Potts."

Millicent raised her eyebrows. "I beg your pardon?"

"Ted Potts. Otherwise known as Daddy Rhythm." He held out his hand. "Pleased to make your acquaintance Mrs Captain."

"Fridlington."

"What?"

"My name is Fridlington, Mrs Fridlington."

"I thought you said it was Mrs Captain?"

"I said I was the wife of Mr Captain."

Daddy Rhythm thought he understood. "Got you. You kept your maiden name. For professional reasons I suppose. Are you in the business?"

Millicent was about to make another attempt at putting Daddy Rhythm right but felt that enough time had been wasted on the cretin already. Daddy Rhythm's hand was still suspended in mid-air waiting for something to shake, however Millicent had always considered disc-jockeys to be trade, and a highly dubious trade at that, and she never shook hands with tradesmen on principle - apart from the question of social class one never knew where their hands had been - so ignoring his hand she got straight down to business. "Those loudspeakers are rather large, aren't they," she said, in a tone which made it abundantly clear she didn't regard the dimensions of the four feet six inches high by two feet wide towers of power as a virtue.

"Two thousand watts RMS each," said Daddy Rhythm, proudly. "Delivering a hundred and twenty decibels of pure pulsating rhythm when I crank up the amps to eleven," he continued, indicating the three amplifiers holding up his quadruple deck CD player. Millicent had no idea how loud a decibel was but a hundred and twenty of them sounded far too many for her liking and her expression said as much. "It'll blow your mind," added Daddy Rhythm, confirming her fears.

"I don't wish to have my mind blown, thank you very much. And I'm quite sure the Mayor doesn't either."

Daddy Rhythm was immediately sympathetic. "Well I can understand that. I mean animals have a much higher sense of hearing, don't they."

"Pardon?"

Something suddenly struck Daddy Rhythm. "But won't it be outside in the fields?"

"In the fields?"

"Or in its stable?"

"Won't what be in its stable?"

"Your mare."

"My mare? What mare?"

"The one you said wouldn't want its mind being blown?"

Millicent was fully aware that the average disc-jockey wasn't on the front row when brains were given out, and was in all probability stood at the back sucking his thumb, but she hadn't up until now thought they were quite as thick as Daddy Rhythm appeared to be. "The *Lord* Mayor!" she said. "It is the *Lord* Mayor who will be the guest of honour this evening!"

Daddy Rhythm's eyes lit up. "Will he be wearing his chain? Daddy Rhythm loves all that ceremonial shit. Please tell me he'll be wearing his chain?"

Anxious to get on, Millicent let Daddy Rhythm's use of the word 'shit' go unchallenged for the time being, but made a mental note to come back to it later, and ignoring his request for information about the Mayor's mode of dress that evening she ploughed on. "Returning to the volume of your disco," she said firmly. "You will be required to keep it low, throughout the entire evening."

Daddy Rhythm looked doubtful. "Well you're the boss. But if I do that I won't enjoy myself and if Daddy Rhythm doesn't enjoy himself the chances are you won't enjoy yourself either."

"I will be the judge of what I will and will not enjoy," said Millicent, huffily. "And your enjoyment doesn't enter into the matter. Your job is to provide the music, not to enjoy yourself. So loudspeakers at a low volume throughout the evening, please. And no flashing lights."

Daddy Rhythm could scarcely believe his ears. Was the woman out of her tree? "No flashing lights? But flashing lights is half the fun."

"Then we will settle for half the fun only. She who pays the piper."

"You want a piper? Just leave it to Daddy Rhythm. We had one at the gig I did last New Year's Eve. Scotch Abdul. An Arab but you'd never know it the way he plays those bagpipes. The man is a maestro, an artist. I have his card," he ended, reaching into the pocket of his lime and lemon coloured velvet waistcoat.

"I don't want a blasted piper!" screamed Millicent, nearing the end of her tether.

"I thought you...?"

Before Daddy Rhythm could maybe suggest bringing along an Albanian who played the didgeridoo accompanied by a Pakistani on a Jew's harp Millicent interrupted him. "Well I didn't. Now then, what type of music do you intend to play?"

Daddy Rhythm spread his hands. "There we won't have a problem. There things will be cool. I do Soul, Hip-hop, Garage, Rap, House, some Lord Nose and the Bogies...."

"No thank you to the last," Millicent sniffed, "I could have had them in person instead of you had I so desired."

Daddy Rhythm's surprise at Millicent's vetoing the flashing lights was as nothing compared to the shock he received on hearing that she'd shunned Lord Nose and the Bogies. "And you turned them down? Lord Nose and the Bogies? Are you mad? They're the next big thing, Mrs Captain."

"Fridlington."

"Sorry, couldn't remember that. Mrs Captain is easier, I'll call you that."

Millicent stamped her foot. "You will call me Mrs Fridlington!"

"Right. No need to lose it, doll. But you really should have gone with Lord Nose and the Bogies if you don't mind me saying so. They're already enormous on the underground scene."

"Under the ground is the best place for them, by the sound of them. Six feet under it."

"Oh don't say that Mrs Friglington...."

"Fridlington!"

"Whatever. No, Lord Nose and the Bogies are the real deal. Have you heard their 'D'you Fancy a Shag'?"

Millicent shuddered. "No and I'm quite sure I don't want to."

Daddy Rhythm was undeterred. "You must check it out. And their 'I Don't Give a Toss'. That's even better if anything; although I must admit it takes a bit more listening to, it's not quite as immediately accessible as 'D'you Fancy a Shag'. I'll give it a spin for you as soon as I've set up my rig, see what you think."

"You most certainly will not!" said Millicent, and turned her mind to more appropriate music for a golf club dance. "Do you have the 'Veleta' amongst your collection?"

"Who are they?" said Daddy Rhythm, wrinkling his brow. "They must be new on the scene if Daddy Rhythm hasn't heard of them. Are they hot?"

"It's not a they, it's a dance, an olde-tyme dance. You do have olde-tyme dance music?"

Daddy Rhythm thought for a moment. "Well I think I've got an Abba record somewhere. 'Dancing Queen'. I play it for a laugh sometimes when I'm pissed."

At this point in the proceedings Millicent almost dispensed with the services of Daddy Rhythm in favour of getting her old Dansette record player down from the loft and bringing that along to provide the music for the evening's dancing, but then decided that if she were to provide the records and give Daddy Rhythm very clear instructions as to what would and would not be played, and keep a close eye on him throughout the evening, they would probably manage to get through it without too much damage being done.

There was one last subject to be broached. "What will you be wearing?" she asked, mindful that the last time they'd had a disco the disc- jockey had changed into an ape costume halfway through the evening and had almost given one of the older lady members a heart attack when he'd jumped out at her waving a banana as she came out of the ladies' toilet, and had caused another lady, on her way to the toilet, to head for it at a greater speed than had been the case beforehand.

"Again you will have nothing to worry about on that score." Daddy Rhythm indicated his sleeveless waistcoat, purple T- shirt and red leggings. "I'll be dressed exactly as you see me now. Except I'll be wearing earrings."

—⁓—

Jason was lagging behind, or making every effort to, given that he was now tied by the wrists to Garland's golf trolley, thanks to Harris's spare shoelaces.

Garland felt the resistance on his trolley due to Jason's reluctance to follow and tugged sharply on the handle causing the laces to dig into the youngster's wrists, making him cry out in pain. Without checking his stride Garland looked over his shoulder, glared at him and snapped, "Well keep up then and it won't happen, will it!"

"You've no right doing this to me," said Jason, aggressively. "Look at my wrists, they're all red."

"All the more reason for you to keep up then, isn't it. And think yourself lucky it isn't your arse that's red," said Garland, giving the trolley another vicious yank just to let Jason know who was the boss.

Jason yelped again. "You'd better let me go," he warned. "I'm telling you!"

"And I'm telling you I'll let you go when we've finished the ninth hole. And even when I do let you go it will only be to hand you over to someone who will detain you until such time as you can be handed over to the police."

"My dad's a policeman," said Jason.

Jason had come back with this far too quickly to fool Garland. "Yes and I'm Father Christmas. Now keep up; and don't complain about your sore wrists if you don't."

Although hurting in both mind and body Jason wasn't over-concerned with his plight. He had the means of escape in his trousers pocket, and just as soon as Garland's attention was drawn away from him for long enough he would use it and be off.

—◈—

Club champion and scratch golfer Graham Southfield opened his eyes and looked at the clock. Twenty to ten. He would have to be get up fairly soon and make the short trip to Jessica's, he didn't want to keep his lady love waiting.

It was Southfield's third extra-marital affair and by far the most satisfying of the three. Not in the sense of sexual gratification – the first two liaisons had been every bit as sexually satisfying as the current one in that respect – but because for the first time, when he was having sex, he felt safe while he was having it.

Throughout his two previous affairs Southfield had been a nervous lover. Whenever he and his mistress had made love he had never been completely comfortable, had never once been able to rid himself entirely of the dread of being caught *en flagrant* by a jealous husband, with the concomitant trouble this would inevitably bring with it. It was his greatest fear.

The only time he had felt anything even approaching comfortable was on the occasion he had taken his first lover Gaynor to London for the weekend – she making the excuse she was visiting the Ideal Homes Exhibition, he telling his wife he was going to the final test match at the Oval – but even then he hadn't felt all that comfortable.

90

On the face of it the dirty weekend in the capital was as safe as houses. To start with they would be about a hundred and fifty miles away from Gaynor's husband, so the chance of his accidentally chancing upon the lovers was virtually non-existent. In addition Gaynor had assured him that her husband would be perfectly happy on his own that weekend as he wanted to finish installing their new kitchen. Furthermore her visit to the Ideal Homes Exhibition wouldn't raise any eyebrows – particularly, thought Southfield, the eyebrows of a husband who would rather spend the weekend installing a new kitchen than making love to his gorgeous wife - as she was in the habit of making a pilgrimage to that very exhibition every year.

Southfield's alibi was equally watertight. Next to golf, cricket was his sport of choice, and he always had at least a couple of days at one or other of the test matches every year. In addition, and making the detection of the assignation even more unlikely than it already was, neither his wife nor Gaynor's husband knew where they would be staying, both Southfield and Gaynor having told their respective spouses that due to being informed at the last moment of a fire at the hotel they wouldn't now be able to stay where they had planned and would have to find accommodation when they arrived in London.

Despite all this Southfield still worried about being discovered, and in particular being discovered whilst 'on the job', as he put it. It was a chance in a million, he knew, but he also knew that chances in a million have a habit of coming up, you only had to look at the National Lottery to appreciate that; apparently the odds of hitting the jackpot were fourteen million to one but people still hit it every week. Granted, he and Gaynor were many miles from London and Gaynor's husband would be making merry with the DIY, but suppose hubby were to cut himself or something and had to be rushed to hospital and he needed a blood transfusion, and he turned out to be a very rare blood group, and he told the doctors that his wife was the same blood group but she was somewhere in London, he didn't know where, and the doctors told the police, and the police had a photograph of her put on the television news, and a maid at the hotel they were staying at saw the news and recognised Gaynor from the photograph and informed the manager, who informed the police, who raced round to their hotel in a squad car and burst into the room at the precise moment he'd reached the vinegar stroke with Gaynor - and one of the policemen, a puritan and a stickler where extra-marital affairs were concerned, had then informed Gaynor's husband of the affair and who, instead of finishing off the kitchen, had set about finishing him off?

Southfield was a self-admitted coward when it came to fisticuffs, and there was no doubt that if he ever found himself in a situation where physical violence to his person looked likely it was a racing certainty he would make no attempt to defend himself but would run for his life. If he were to be caught Southfield just hoped it would be with his trousers down rather than off, but even to have to flee trouser-less would be more preferable than having the benefit of trousers but being duffed up by a jealous husband. The question of being caught by a jealous husband was a constant worry to him during his relationship with Gaynor, and his second lover, Helena.

However it was most unlikely to happen with Jessica, his third and current lover. For there was little chance of Jessica's husband ever finding out they were having an affair, and no chance whatsoever of his being caught in bed with her and being forced to make a run for it, with or without trousers. This was because Jessica's husband, like Southfield himself, was a member of Sunnymere Golf Club. Southfield's ploy was simple but effective, worked out even before he had even met Jessica, and put into practice soon after he had first set eyes on her and knew she was the one.

Indeed the subterfuge could only have worked with the wife of a golfer. The plan was simplicity itself. Whenever there was a competition, which was mostly once a week, usually a Saturday or Sunday, Southfield would wait until Jessica's husband had put down his name on the starting times list. Having noted the elected time he would then enter his own name. If Jessica's husband had put his name down for the morning round Southfield would put his name down for the afternoon round, and vice versa. Therefore on the day of the competition once Jessica's husband had started out on his round Southfield knew it would be several hours before he returned home. These hours Southfield would spend in his bed with Jessica.

This arrangement meant that he and Jessica only got to make love once a week, but after seven days apart it only served to heighten their ardour and increase the enjoyment of their illicit union.

An added bonus was that Jessica's house bordered the golf course, which meant that while her husband was toiling on the adjacent fairways Southfield was toiling between his wife's thighs, an embellishment that appealed to Southfield's baser instincts and added a certain frisson to the occasion whilst still leaving him absolutely safe from detection.

Southfield had heard of the maxim that where extra-marital affairs are concerned it is considered prudent not to do it on your own doorstep, and subscribed to the principle wholeheartedly. In fact he had made sure that his two previous lovers lived several miles distant from *chez* Southfield. It was no small irony then that now he finally felt safe not only was he doing it on his own doorstep but revelling in doing so.

Now, still in bed after a late night drinking session at the Grim Jogger the previous evening, he looked at his watch on the bedside locker. Almost ten to ten. Time to get out of his bed, make the short walk to Jessica's, and get into her bed.

—ᚱᚱ—

On the eighth green Arbuthnott holed a four-footer for his par. "Yes!" he cried, punching the air once again as the ball dropped into the hole. "That makes me two over after eight holes." He retrieved his ball and kissed it. "That's a net twenty seven. I'm going to murder this."

"I thought I knew what crowing was," said Chapman, in mock surprise. "I didn't know what crowing was. Not a bit of it. I still may not know what it is. I suspect I'll really find out what crowing is if by some almighty fluke you happen to win."

"Do I detect a hint of jealousy in your banter, Gerry?" said Arbuthnott, with a patronising smile.

"It's only a game, Arby," Chapman scoffed.

"Only a game, Gerry? That isn't what you said when you won the Sunnymere Cup. I seem to remember you claiming it was a sport then. I was at the presentation. 'When you roll in that putt on the eighteenth to win there can be no finer feeling in sport', you said."

"That's when you win," Bagley chipped in. "It's a sport when you win but only a game when you lose, isn't it Gerry."

"Well today it is I who is playing sport and Gerry who is playing a game," said Arbuthnott, irrevocably. "And not a very good game at that."

"We'll see," said Chapman. "There's another ten holes to play; and a lot can happen in ten holes."

—⁂—

Tobin was devastated. "You're sacked," Mr Captain had said. "You can't sack me," Tobin had replied. And Mr Captain couldn't sack him, he was sure of that. But he was equally sure that Mr Captain would very easily be able to talk the General Committee into sacking him, which, Mr Captain had then gone on to inform him, was precisely what he was going to do, and just as soon as he could call an extraordinary committee meeting. Tobin's feet wouldn't touch, Mr Captain had assured him.

So that was it. He was on his way out, it was a done deal. Golf clubs did not take kindly to their professional announcing to the captain's wife that one of the lady members didn't have any tits, while at the same time groping his assistant's tits, even though Darren's mammaries were artificial. It was only Mrs Fridlington's word against his of course, but he knew which one of them the General Committee would believe, and it certainly wasn't the Sunnymere golf professional.

There was Darren of course, a witness to the incident; but a witness for the prosecution rather than the defence if he were to tell the truth, and even if he could persuade Darren into lying for him who would take the word of a callow youth before that of the wife of Mr Captain?

Tobin considered his future, and it was bleak. No longer would he have the rich pickings for very little work which had been his lot at Sunnymere for the past few years. Instead there would be nothing ahead of him but the hard graft that came with having to slowly build up a new client base at a new club. That was assuming he could get a new club!

There were always jobs to be had as golf club professionals of course, but most golf clubs liked their professional to play a little golf now and then, indeed many of them demanded that he not only played the game but played it to a reasonably high standard. Which lets me out, thought Tobin, ruefully.

Add to that the fact that the reason he had been booted out of Sunnymere would soon become common knowledge, the healthy club golf grapevine seeing to that, and his chances of landing a new job were slimmer than a catwalk model with anorexia.

There was no doubt about it, it was a disaster of the first water. And there was not a thing he could do about it.

G Venables (11)
J Jenkins (16)
D Davis (18)

The many hours spent by Denis Davis's parents agonising over what Christian name to confer on their beautiful baby son were entirely wasted, as ever since he had taken up the game of golf at the age of twelve he had been known to all and sundry as Dogleg Davis.

Davis, unsurprisingly, had been given his nickname because he was in the habit of playing almost all the holes at Sunnymere as though they were doglegs. This was of course by accident rather than by design, and caused by an exaggerated in-to-out swing that resulted in either a massive push shot or a violent hook, depending upon whether the face of his club happened to be square or closed when it came into contact with the ball. (Fortunately it was only rarely open at impact, for those balls were rarely ever seen again.)

Fourteen of the holes at Sunnymere are either dead straight, or as near to straight as makes no difference, whilst the other four are doglegs. Naturally, due to the idiosyncratic way he hit the ball, Dogleg Davis played all the straight holes as though they were doglegs and all the dogleg holes as though they were straight. This resulted in his covering much more mileage than would the average golfer during his round of golf, and was the reason that led him into making the rather startling claim which he now made to his playing partners Jeff Jenkins and Guy Venables as they waited to drive off at the first tee.

"I reckon I'm a better golfer than Tiger Woods," he proclaimed, without so much as a trace of doubt, irony or humour in his voice.

"What?" said Jenkins, not because he hadn't heard what Davis had claimed but because he couldn't believe what he had heard.

"Are you sure you don't mean Tiger Tim, Dogleg?" said Venables, fully believing what he had heard, as he was wearing the very latest in hearing aids, but placing very little credence in Davis's preposterous claim. He was about to continue, mentioning that the shop from which he had purchased his hearing-aid, Eyes and Ears Direct, also did excellent spectacles, and to suggest to Davis he could do worse than purchase a pair as he was quite obviously in urgent need of ocular assistance, but before he could Davis had re-affirmed his claim.

"No, really," he said, taking a very un-Tiger Woods-ish practice swing, which didn't even threaten the dandelion he had been aiming at, far less decapitate it. "I've worked it out."

"Give over, Dogleg," Jenkins scoffed.

"You're having a laugh," said Venables.

Davis was adamant. "All right I'll prove it. How many strokes do you reckon it would take Tiger Woods to go round Sunnymere ?"

Jenkins looked thoughtful. After a moment or so he said, "It's difficult to say. I mean he's a big powerful lad the Tiger isn't he, he hits the ball a country mile."

"That makes two of us then, because I hit the ball a country mile too. And I go round in about eighty eight on a good day."

"Yes but ninety nine times out of a hundred Tiger Woods hits the ball in the general direction he wants it to go," said Venables, "Whereas you usually go from tee to green via the duck pond, the car park and Disneyland."

Davis however refused to be put off his claim. "That is completely immaterial to my argument. So what score do you think Tiger would go round in then?"

The two gave the matter a little more thought. Jenkins was the first to give his opinion. "Well Sunnymere is par seventy, standard scratch sixty eight. Not for the likes of Tiger Woods though. He'd murder the short par fours, he'd almost drive the green on some of them. About sixty four I would think; on average."

"Agreed?" asked Davis, turning to Venables.

"Sixty three," said Venables, after a further moment's consideration. "I think he'd go round in sixty three."

"All right then, sixty three," conceded Davis. "And how long is the Sunnymere course?"

"Six thousand five hundred and something," said Jenkins.

Venables checked the exact distance on his scorecard. "Six thousand six hundred and thirty four yards off the back tees."

"And what length would you say I play it at?"

"You, Dogleg? Well you're all over the place, aren't you," said Jenkins. "About nine thousand yards I should think. Minimum."

"On a good day," added Venables. "Up to eleven thousand on a bad one."

"All right then, we'll split the difference and say ten," said Davis. "Right. So Tiger Woods goes round a six thousand six hundred and thirty yards golf course in sixty three shots. Which means he takes..." He took out a pocket calculator and punched the numbers in. "...one shot every one hundred and five yards. I go round a ten thousand yard course in eighty eight shots. I take..." He used the calculator again. "....one shot about every hundred and thirteen yards. So I get eight yards more out of each shot I take than Tiger does. Obviously making me the better golfer."

Jenkins and Venables pondered on this for a moment or two. Finally Venables spoke. "So how come you're a long distance lorry driver on about four hundred quid a week and Tiger Woods is well on the way to his first billion?"

"I haven't worked that out yet," said Davis.

—⁓—

After their approach shots to the third green Armitage's ball lay about twenty feet from the hole, Stock's ball a similar distance, whilst Grover's ball was about ten feet away.

"Who's away?" said Armitage, weighing up the positions of the respective balls.

"There can't be a lot in it," said Stock.

Armitage paced out the distance from his ball to the hole, did the same for Stock's ball and announced his verdict. "It's just about me. By about a dick's length."

Grover cocked an ear. "Dicks again, Trevor."

"What?"

"About a dick's length? You can't keep your mind off dicks for five minutes, can you."

Armitage brushed it off. "It's just a figure of speech."

"It's just a figure of your speech you mean. Anyone else would have said 'By about six inches'. Or whatever the length of a dick happens to be."

"Six and three quarter inches," said Armitage, quick as a flash. "On average. Erect. According to my information."

"Yes well that's bound to be right then, isn't it. Because I don't think for one moment there's any chance of the information supplied by somebody who thinks about dicks all day long to be anything but absolutely spot on."

Armitage protested. "Who thinks about dicks all day? I don't."

"No, of course you don't, Trevor," said Grover, with a knowing wink at Stock.

Armitage noticed the wink. "Well I don't," he insisted, and proceeded to qualify this contention. "I wasn't thinking about dicks when we were walking up to the green together just now and you were talking to Gerard about butterflies. I was thinking about Paris, because I'm off there next week for the weekend."

"Me and the wife went there the other week," said Stock. "I'd never been before."

"I've been a couple of times," said Grover. "What did you think to it?"

"Great. It was really enjoyable. The Louvre, the Left Bank, the Eiffel Tower ..."

"That was built as a phallic symbol, you know, the Eiffel Tower," said Armitage.

Grover rolled his eyes. "What did I tell you? What did I just say?"

"What?"

"Dicks again. Eiffel Tower, phallic symbol, dicks again."

"Well it *was* built as a phallic symbol," protested Armitage. "It's not my fault the French built it like a big dick, you know what they're like. Anyway I was only saying, can't you say anything now?"

"I'm fast beginning to think you can't say anything if it doesn't include dicks in it," said Grover.

—⚏—

After Mr Captain had seen Davis, Jenkins and Venables on their way he noticed the Arbuthnott threesome walking down the ninth fairway on their way to the green, so started to make his way over to the beer tent to welcome them after they'd completed the hole.

Mr Captain was very happy with the way things had gone thus far. There had been a couple of blips – the unpleasant business with that naked youth chasing after one of the members for some reason or another, he didn't know what and he didn't want to know, and the disappointment of the band being double-booked and having to make do with a disco – but certainly nothing serious enough to spoil his day significantly.

The next blip not serious enough to spoil his day significantly, but a blip he could have well done without, happened just short of the bunker by the side of the eighteenth green when he looked up at the skies again to check for signs of any change in the weather. He had done this maybe a couple of dozen times since Ifield had warned him of Fred the Weatherman's dire forecast, and he'd come to the conclusion that Fred the Weatherman didn't know what he was talking about as every time he had checked he'd seen nothing but cloudless skies and the sun. Which was exactly what he saw now. Then he saw stars. Lots of stars. When he trod on the business end of the rake he'd taken out of the bunker about an hour ago and the other end of it shot up and gave him a nasty crack on the nose. "Damn!" he said, which was the nearest he ever got to swearing, and only then when he was severely pressed.

He felt his nose. It was wet. He looked at his hand. There was blood on it. He took out his handkerchief and dabbed the blood away, then felt his nose again, gingerly. He breathed a sigh of relief as it didn't appear to be broken. Being hit on the nose by the rake had spoiled his day just a little but if the blow had broken his nose it would have spoiled it considerably. An hour later he would have happily accepted a broken arm, a broken leg and possibly even a broken neck in exchange for what was about to befall him.

—⁓—

No more than ten minutes after Tobin had realised he could do nothing about Mr Captain getting him the sack he realised he could. He could exact revenge. It wouldn't save him from the sack of course but at least it would wipe the self-satisfied smirk off that tight-arsed twat of a Mr Captain's face. It was just a matter of deciding what form the revenge would take. It would have to be something he couldn't be held responsible for though, something that didn't throw any suspicion on him; it would be difficult enough to obtain another position as a club pro as it already was without accusations of having taken revenge on the captain of his former club being levelled against him. And whatever it was he decided on it would have to be something that could be carried out pretty quickly, because he couldn't see himself being at Sunnymere for very much longer once the extraordinary meeting had sat and announced its verdict. And preferably it should be something that spoiled Mr Captain's day.

Tobin put on his thinking cap. A bomb scare? Possibly. Pretend to be an IRA terrorist, phone up the police and tell them a bomb had been planted in one of the course's seventy three bunkers, guess which, and was due to go off at noon? No. It would spoil Mr Captain's day, no doubt about that, because the course would have to be cleared and all the bunkers checked out; but there was always the outside chance the call might be traced back to him; and apart from that didn't IRA terrorists have a special code they used when they phoned so that the police knew it was a genuine threat and not some crank on the other end of the line?

Allow Mr Captain to enjoy his day, and his evening, then lie in wait for him when he arrived home and give him a bloody good duffing up? Wearing a mask so he couldn't be recognised. No. Too risky again. Mr Captain wasn't likely to put up much of a fight but something might go wrong, the mask might slip off or something, and even if things went to plan he would be a prime suspect, being a soon-to-be ex-employee with a very large axe to grind.

He looked out of the window hoping to find inspiration there. From his shop he could see out onto the lane that wended its way past the back of the clubhouse. Two young girls in riding breeches carrying large black plastic buckets under their arms were walking past on their way to the horse riding stables a half mile or so up the lane. He often saw young girls carrying buckets on their way to the stables and the only interest he had ever taken in them, apart from admiring their firm young bottoms as they walked past, was to wonder what it was they carried in the buckets. Oats for their horse? A brush with which to groom it? A spare tampon? All he knew was that whenever he saw young girls on the way to their horses they always carried buckets. He had once had the thought that you didn't need to own a horse to convince someone you were a horse owner, you merely had to walk around carrying a black plastic bucket under your arm.

The girls passed by and after he had appreciated their bottoms and imagined cupping them in his hands and fondling them he was about to re-apply himself to the task of coming up with a suitable form of revenge on Mr Captain when a tractor from the stables passed by travelling in the opposite direction; and the combination of the tractor and the girls' bottoms gave him exactly the thing he was looking for, and Mr Captain's day was well on the way to being well and truly spoiled.

—◊—

When Garland had been teeing off at the fourth, and Harris and Ifield had been watching him, Jason had taken the opportunity to find out if despite being tied to Garland's trolley he could still get at the penknife in his trousers' pocket. He smiled to himself when he found that with a little effort he could. He already knew his chance of escape would come sooner rather than later as he had often seen the members of Sunnymere playing golf and knew it wouldn't be very long before one of them lost their ball and the others helped him find it.

The chance to escape presented itself when Harris's sliced approach shot ended up in the azaleas about forty yards to the right of the fourth green. Garland had hit the green with his own approach shot and after pulling Jason along with his trolley to the green's edge he now parked them there whilst he went to Harris's assistance. No sooner was his back turned than Jason took out his penknife, cut through the laces binding him to the trolley, and was off long before Garland became aware of what was happening. In fact if Jason hadn't called out "I'll get you for this you bald-headed old bugger!" before running off it would have been even longer before Garland found out. The vice captain gave chase but not being in the best of condition these days he soon realised the futility of it and gave up, contenting himself with waving a fist at the departing Jason and shouting that he would fucking crucify him if he ever laid hands on him again.

—⁓—

After leaving Daddy Rhythm Millicent had proceeded to the beer tent, where she was to help out when the golfers called in for their drink with Mr Captain. Assisting her in this task would be the lady captain Mrs Jordan, who had already entrenched herself in the beer tent when Millicent arrived, even though it was still some time away from when the first of the golfers were due to arrive.

Millicent had long thought it would have been more apt if Mrs Jordan had been called Mrs Gordon, judging by the amount of the gin of that name she drank, and would have much preferred one of the other ladies to help her out, or indeed done without any help at all if the only help on offer came in the shape of the lady captain. However Mrs Jordan had insisted and Millicent could hardly turn her down.

The reason for the lady captain's insistence and for her premature arrival in the tent became apparent to Millicent the moment she entered the beer tent and noted that already one of the bottles of gin was a third empty. "It spilled as I was putting the optic on," the lady captain explained, with an innocent smile, on noticing Millicent looking at the bottle with raised eyebrows.

"Yes and your throat just happened to be in the way before it could hit the floor," thought Millicent, but said, "What a shame, Lady Captain. I know they can be a bit tricky so perhaps you'd better let me put the optic on the next bottle of gin when the present one is empty, I seem to have the knack."

"Of course," said the lady captain sweetly, at the same time making plans that would ensure Millicent would be putting the optic on the next bottle without too much delay.

P Norris (4)
R Oates (5)
S Pemberton (7)

Paul Norris, Ray Oates and Simon Pemberton teed off at the first then made their way, abreast of each other, for they were accomplished golfers, down the fairway. They were also accomplished wits.

"Corey Pavin," said Norris

"Fuzzy Zoeller," said Oates

"Howard Twitty," said Pemberton.

—m—

After taking a four at the par four ninth to remain two over par gross at the halfway stage Arbuthnott began to believe for the first time that he could win the competition. He had said as much on the way to the first tee, and had meant what he'd said, but he had done this on numerous occasions in the past but not really believed it; it had been said as a way of finding inspiration, of geeing himself up into making some sort of a show of it. The difference this time was that it seemed to be working; instead of his challenge petering out after a few holes (or not even starting, as it did the day he tried out his new Lee Trevino swing and went nine off the tee at the first after hitting his first three attempts out of bounds and accomplishing an air shot with his fourth attempt), he seemed on this occasion to be very much heading for a win. Now, anxious to keep his round going, he was more than glad they wouldn't be stopping off at the beer tent for a drink with Mr Captain, with the consequent risk of his concentration being thrown out of kilter.

"You must be in with some sort of a chance if you can manage to keep it together, Arby," said Bagley, as they left the green and started to make their way over to the tenth tee some eighty yards away.

"It's early days yet," said Arbuthnott cautiously, not wishing to tempt providence, but also not to give Chapman the opportunity to accuse him of crowing again.

Chapman was completely unconvinced by Arbuthnott's apparent and unexpected show of modesty. "*Very* early days, for a crower," he said. "I remember once being in a similar position after nine holes myself."

"You must have a bloody good memory," said Arbuthnott, unable to resist giving Chapman a bit of his own back.

Standing outside the beer tent, waiting to play mine host to Arbuthnott, Bagley and Chapman, Mr Captain was wondering why they were heading towards the tenth tee and not towards him. Could they have forgotten? Surely not. Surely they wouldn't have overlooked such a long-standing tradition as a drink with the captain at the halfway stage of the Captain's Prize competition? He raised an arm aloft and hailed them. "I say!" The threesome didn't hear him, or if they did they chose to ignore him. He shouted again, this time at the top of his voice, so it was quite impossible for them not to hear him. They stopped and looked over in his direction. He beckoned to them to join him. Chapman shook his head and all three turned and continued on their way to the tee. Totally bemused, Mr Captain shouted again. "I say!" The three stopped, turned resignedly to face him again, but made no attempt to join him. Mr Captain reluctantly cast himself in the role of Mohammad and made for the mountain, radiating concern.

"What's going on, gentlemen? Surely you're having a drink with me?" he said on arrival.

"No thank you, Mr Captain, we'd rather not," said Chapman, rather abruptly.

"You aren't?" Mr Captain's main concern up until then had been how he could keep everyone down to one drink; this was something he hadn't bargained for. "But whyever not?"

Chapman shrugged as if to say whether or not they had a drink with the captain on Captain's Day was a matter of little importance.

Arbuthnott shrugged but at least had the decency to accompany the gesture with a wan smile.

Bagley was more forthcoming. "We've decided not to bother with the beer tent this year, Mr Captain."

"Not to bother with it?"

"If it's all the same to you."

"But it isn't all the same to me."

"Well all right then, if it isn't all the same to you," said Chapman, the more blunt of the three. "We still don't want a drink with you."

"But... I don't understand?"

"Well it's the no swearing rule if you must know, Mr Captain," said Arbuthnott.

"The no swearing rule?"

"We think it stinks," said Chapman, in case Mr Captain should be in any doubt.

"Neither my playing partners nor I particularly want to swear," Bagley explained. "Personally I never do. But we don't much like being told that we can't. We see it as a golfer's prerogative and something that is almost bound to happen with most golfers occasionally. So I'm afraid we won't be having a drink with you, in protest."

Faced with this sudden spanner in the works, Mr Captain was at a loss as to what stance to adopt. However after a few seconds' thought he decided that as it was only three out of a total of a hundred and fifty golfers taking part in the Captain's Day competition who wouldn't be partaking of his hospitality that he would opt for a cavalier approach. "I see," he pouted. "Well of course that is your decision to make. But it is a pretty misguided, not to say petty, decision, if I may say so."

"You may, but that's the way we feel about it," said Chapman.

"Well it's no skin off my nose; it certainly doesn't matter to me that you refuse to have a drink with me. All the more for the others taking part, say I." With that Mr Captain turned smartly on his heel and started to make his way back to the beer tent.

"There won't be any others," Chapman called after him.

Mr Captain stopped in his tracks. He turned to face Chapman. "What? What do you mean?"

"I'm afraid all the members feel exactly the same way about it as we do," said Bagley. "None of them will be having a drink with you."

From being in the position when having three of the members refuse to accept his hospitality in the beer tent would be no skin off his nose a whole noseful of skin now suddenly shed itself from Mr Captain's proboscis. He was completely crushed. "N....none of them?"

"You made your bed," said Chapman, before turning and heading for the tenth tee. Arbuthnott and Bagley fell in behind him.

Mr Captain watched them go, completely at a loss. If what they had said was true it would be disastrous. Apart from it completely spoiling his day what on earth would the Lord Mayor think if he found out that the members of the club held him in such low esteem that they even refused to have a drink with him, and a free one at that? He saw his chances of becoming a town councillor and a future Lord Mayor dwindling rapidly. Something would have to be done about it, and pretty quickly too if his day wasn't to be spoiled.

—⚒—

"How much do you want?" asked the man on the other end of the telephone.

Tobin told him. Then changed his mind and doubled the amount, just to make sure. Muck or nettles he thought, then smiled to himself at the allusion.

"And where do you want it delivered to?"

Tobin told him.

"What? Are you sure?"

"I've never been surer," said Tobin.

—⚒—

"Father," said Millicent, positively.

"Father?" echoed Mr Captain, then added, doubtfully, "Your father?"

"Well of course. I'm sure he'd be only too happy to help."

On discovering from the Arbuthnott threesome that the entire field was going to refuse to have a drink with him Mr Captain had returned to the beer tent to counsel Millicent. Two heads were better than one and it was clear that some pretty quick thinking would have to be done if he were to overcome the latest crisis to be dropped in his lap. However by offering her father as a solution to the problem it was clear to Mr Captain that Millicent wasn't yet thinking along lines that might prove fruitful. "It is golfers we are short of, Millicent," he said in reply to his wife's suggestion. "Golfers seen to be having a drink on me during the Mayoral visit. How on earth can your father help? He's never played golf in his life."

"He doesn't have to have played golf. All he has to do is stand here with you in the beer tent and have a drink; I'm sure he knows how to do that."

Mr Captain wasn't. As far as he could remember Millicent's father didn't drink, her mother having seen to that. He pointed this out. "I thought you father was a teetotaller?"

"What? Well he is," said Millicent, a little cross. Her husband could be so pedantic sometimes. "There are soft drinks, aren't there? He can have a soft drink. I'll get him to bring along a couple of his friends, they can pretend to be golfers too. There, there's your threesome."

It seemed like a possible way round the problem but Mr Captain was still a little dubious. "He'll be all right, will he, your father?"

"What do you mean, all right?"

"Well, since your mother...I mean he hasn't long been a widower has he, and..."

"Mother passed away almost three months ago, Henry. And it isn't as though we're asking father to scale Mount Everest, is it? All we're asking him to do is have a drink with you. So do I go for him or don't I?"

Mr Captain still wasn't totally comfortable with the idea but had no better solution to the problem. "I suppose it will be all right," he said, but in the hope that he would come up with something better before the Lord Mayor arrived.

New member Jeremy Bramwell's topped tee shot at the first wasn't the most distinguished opening shot of the day, but then neither was it the worst. (That dubious honour went to Peter Keaney, whose ball sliced off the toe of his driver and hit one of the tee markers before ricocheting back behind him, over the road and through the open clubhouse door, whereupon the greens chairman Maurice Maidment, a man known for his opportunism as well as for his parsimony, immediately claimed it as a 'find' and popped it in his blazer pocket whilst no one was looking.)

"A Sally Gunnell," observed Terry Plumstone, following the flight, or lack of it, of Bramwell's ball, which had attained an altitude of no more than two feet at its highest point as it bounded down the fairway like a miniature Barnes Wallis bouncing bomb.

"What?" said Bramwell.

"You've just hit a Sally Gunnell."

"A Sally Gunnell?"

"Ugly but a good runner," explained Plumstone.

"Ugly?" said Bramwell, surprised. "Sally Gunnell? I find the lady quite becoming."

Healey gaped. "You're talking about the runner? The ex-Olympic hurdler? Did a stint as a TV commentator? Absolute crap at it?"

"But of course."

"Are you sure you're all right, Jeremy?" Plumstone enquired, in mock concern. "I could send for a doctor."

"Probably the heat's got to him, Terry," said Healey.

Bramwell shook his head, quite bemused. "I really don't understand you two. What on earth is wrong with

110

Sally Gunnell? She's one of the most attractive women I've ever set eyes on."

"I'll send for that doctor then," said Plumstone.

Healey now began to suspect where Bramwell might be coming from. After all the Olympic gold medallist was possessed of a slim, toned figure and a healthy tan, and if you were to disregard her face and her appalling estuary accent it might then just be possible to believe that someone could find her attractive, especially if it were someone who placed more store on a woman's figure than her looks and diction. "Well if you put a bag over her head and gagged her you might just be able to say she was attractive," he conceded to Bramwell.

"No, it isn't just her shapely body," said Bramwell. "I find her quite pretty."

Healey just couldn't believe it. "Quite pretty? Sally Gunnell? She's got a face like a bag of spanners."

"On the contrary, I've always thought her most fetching."

Shaking his head in disbelief and saying to himself that it takes all sorts, Healey let the matter lie and took his place on the tee. He was about to drive off when the sound of a car pulling up behind the tee disturbed his concentration. He turned in time to see, alighting from the car, what was without any doubt the ugliest woman he had ever seen in his life. She now waved and called to Bramwell. "Jeremy!"

"What is it, darling?" said Bramwell, a little concerned, going over to her.

She took an asthma spray from her handbag and held it up. "You forgot this."

"I'd forget my head if it were loose," smiled Bramwell. He indicated Plumstone and Healey. "This is Terry Plumstone and Chris Healey, by the way. Terry and Chris, my wife Daphne."

—⁓—

"The first ones should be along quite soon," said Mrs Quayle, glancing at her watch.

"About ten-thirty if Mr Captain is to be believed," said Mrs Rattray.

"Then let the measuring of the Nearest the Pin competition commence!" announced Mrs Salinas.

The three ladies had taken up position behind the green about five yards back from the putting surface.

It had occurred to Mrs Quayle that the spot the three ladies had chosen, immediately behind the flagstick and clearly visible from the tee some hundred and fifty yards away, might be distracting to a golfer taking his tee shot; however it was also the spot that afforded the ladies the nicest view of the surrounding countryside, and also had the added benefit of the shade of the only tree, so in the matter of selecting a spot from which to operate, and choosing a spot which wouldn't distract the golfers, it was no contest.

Mrs Rattray and Mrs Salinas hadn't even considered the golfers.

Whilst they were waiting for their first customers to arrive Mrs Quayle was leafing through a copy of The Lady, Mrs Rattray was reading Woman's Own, whilst Mrs Salinas was making a daisy chain.

"This is a bit like yours, Miriam," said Mrs Rattray, showing Mrs Quayle a page in her magazine. "Your new conservatory."

Mrs Quayle pulled a face. "Don't mention conservatories to me. They said it would take three days to install. Three weeks it took them. I told them it only took God a week to make the entire world."

"*And* he took Sunday off," said Mrs Salinas.

"The men who put my conservatory in didn't," said Mrs Quayle. "Hammering and banging away while Bernard and I were trying to read the Sunday papers. It was the first time Bernard has failed to complete the Times crossword in years for all the din. He was quite put out. And then we had to pay them extra for working during the weekend even though it was their own fault they'd got behind with the job in the first place! It was all that tea drinking."

"They were just the same when I was having my lounge extension," sympathised Mrs Salinas. "I spent half the day brewing up for them. I didn't have to warm the teapot, it never got cold. *And* one of them insisted on Earl Grey. Earl Grey indeed!"

"Of course they didn't have conservatories in those days," said Mrs Rattray.

"In what days?" said Mrs Quayle.

"When God made the world. It might have taken him longer than a week to create the world if they'd had conservatories in biblical times and he'd had to provide everyone with a conservatory."

"It would if he'd employed the ones who installed my conservatory to erect them," said Mrs Quayle.

"And they drank tea at the same rate my lot did," agreed Mrs Salinas.

—☠—

Norris, Oates and Pemberton were walking up the second fairway.

"Ron Mediate."

"Chip Beck."

"Duffy Waldorf."

—☠—

Forty minutes had passed since Armitage had eaten the space cake and as yet it had had little or no effect on him. Certainly he didn't feel anything like as relaxed as when he'd taken the previous space cake, nor had his golf improved as his snooker had.

Although he would have much preferred to be burning up the course he wasn't particularly worried about the situation as his brother had warned him that you didn't always get the exact same reaction upon taking a space cake, and for a variety of reasons, the main one being that space cake manufacture wasn't as advanced as, say, Jaffa cake production; to what degree the cannabis had been incorporated into the mixture was apparently a governing factor, as if it hadn't been thoroughly mixed each individual space cake would vary in strength. In arriving at a dosage consistent with one's expectations his brother had therefore advised a suck-it-and-see policy, or rather an eat-it-and-see policy, and if having eaten one space cake you observed that it wasn't enough to bring about the desired effect the remedy was simply to eat another one.

Recalling his brother's advice Armitage reached into his golf bag, took out another space cake, and made short work of it.

—⁓—

In the absence of Millicent, who had left the beer tent to go for her father, and Mr Captain, who had left to return to the first tee to welcome and see off the next group, the Lady Captain took the opportunity to help herself to another generous measure from the gin bottle.

A Adams (5)
B Adams (5)
C Adams (5)

The Adams brothers were far and away Sunnymere's most successful golfers when it came to the winning of prizes. Between them the siblings won almost a quarter of all the club competitions they entered. They could quite easily have won more, but to have been even more successful than they already were might have drawn more attention to them, attention they could do without; for in order to achieve their success they cheated.

A man taking part in a round of golf is largely observed only by his playing partners, and very often not even by them. Because of this it is comparatively easy to cheat at golf, which is why the game is looked upon by those who play it as being as much a test of character as it is a test of one's skill at the game. The methods of cheating are many and diverse; pretending to find your lost ball by the expedient of surreptitiously dropping another ball in the area where the lost ball had been seen to land; improving the lie of your ball in the rough by astute use of the foot; placing your ball nearer the hole when replacing it on the putting surface after having marked it; and many more.

However by far the easiest way to cheat at golf is for the golfer to claim he has taken fewer strokes on a hole than he has actually taken, a sharp pencil turning many a six into a more respectable and less damaging five when a chip and a putt has failed to do the job. Claiming a false number of strokes taken was the only form of cheating employed by the Adams brothers, all other methods of deception, the brothers having tried and tested them, being judged as too reckless and open to discovery.

The main appeal to the Adams brothers of their chosen form of cheating was that there was no possibility whatsoever of them ever being found out, and the reason they could never be found out was because they always played together. That the Adams brothers were identical triplets helped enormously in their deceptions. This was enhanced by their always dressing identically, leastwise when they were on the golf course. And gilded by their carrying identical golf bags containing identical clubs. Quite literally, whenever they were playing golf, it was impossible to tell them apart.

If a golfer were to consistently claim a lower score than he had actually taken it would eventually be noticed by someone, a close watch on that individual would be made by his playing partners and the guilty golfer would eventually be found out and brought to book. Such a close watch could not be made on the Adams triplets, at least not without it being very noticeable, for the stated reason that they always played together. But even if their progress on the golf course could have been monitored it wouldn't have made the slightest difference for the simple fact that although the brothers might for example take a total of eighteen shots between them on a particular hole anyone observing would have no way of knowing for certain how many of the eighteen strokes each individual Adams brother had taken. Given that they had each hit a tee shot and each had holed out on the green, which would account for six of the eighteen strokes, any of the brothers could have recorded a score of anything from two to fourteen, and there was no way of determining the true figure for a particular Adams. As long as the brothers took care that the total number of strokes taken on any one hole equalled the number of strokes taken on that hole by each of them they had nothing to worry about.

Once the Adams triplets realised this they had never looked back, and took their turn to win competitions at their pleasure, and their pleasure was often. The subterfuge didn't always work of course, as they could never be certain what would qualify that day as a winning score - golf being golf it is always possible for someone to have a dream round and come in with a genuine but almost impossibly low score - but more often than not when an Adams brother decided he wanted to win a competition he would win it. The club officials knew that a winning Adams card was as suspicious as a milk bill but there was not a thing they could do about it.

As they all boasted a handicap of five, although ten would have been nearer the mark if their cheating were to be discounted, they took the honour at the first tee in alphabetical order, so Alec teed off first, followed by Brian, then Charles.

On the occasion of Captain's Day it had been decided amongst the brothers that Alec would win the competition, Brian already having won the President's Putter and Charles the Club Championship that year. Alec's opening drive was a poor one, a slice into the rough on the right. His pitching wedge second got him out of the rough but only a matter of a few yards down the fairway. He hooked his three iron third shot into the left hand pot bunker guarding the green. His first attempt at a recovery shot hit the lip of the bunker and rolled back into the sand. His second attempt got him out of the sand but he thinned the ball slightly and it cleared the putting surface, coming to rest in the pretty on the opposite side of the green. His sixth shot, a chip back onto the green, left his ball twelve feet from the pin. He just missed the putt and tapped in for an eight.

"Good four," said Brian.

"Cheers," said Alec.

—⁂—

Armitage was beginning to doubt the wisdom of eating a second space cake and was now wishing he'd given the first one a little longer to start working, as it was becoming increasingly clear that whilst one space cake may or may not have been enough two space cakes were one space cake too many. The first untoward thing happened when he had taken hold of the flagstick at the seventh green and turned his head towards Stock to ask him if he wanted it removed or tended. Even though his brain was becoming more scrambled by the second Armitage knew it was beyond dispute that he had moved his head in Stock's direction – this was borne out by the fact that he was now looking directly at him - yet his head still seemed to be where it had been before he moved it. He now turned his head back to see if it would cure the problem. It didn't, because although he was now facing in the direction in which he had originally been facing, his head felt as if it were still looking at Stock. It was just as though he had two heads.

It is thought by some that two heads are better than one, in fact Mr Captain had voiced that very sentiment only minutes before when discussing with his wife the problem he faced vis-à-vis the boycott of the beer tent, however Armitage would have put up a strong argument against this maxim, as from that moment on his two heads, far from being better than one, started to become considerably worse than one.

—⁓—

"Lonny Long the Second."

"Davis Love the Third."

"Fred Fuckem the Fourth."

"You can't have that," protested Norris, immediately. "Not allowed. You can't start making them up until we're playing the fourth."

"I thought this was the fourth?" said Pemberton.

"It's the third."

"Sorry," said Pemberton, then after a second or two's thought, "Bo Weekley."

—⁓—

Dogleg Davis had hooked his tee shot at the fourth onto the tenth fairway, which ran more or less parallel to the fourth. Ploughing through the expanse of rough that separated the two mown areas he passed Fidler, who had sliced his tee shot at the tenth onto the fourth fairway.

"Perhaps we could play each other's balls?" said Davis, jokingly. "Save our legs."

"Bollocks," said Fidler, which was not the response Davis had come to expect from a fellow golfer upon making an obviously light-hearted remark.

1 1 8

Walking up the left side of the fourth fairway towards his own ball Venables noticed Fidler heading his way. As Fidler was renowned for being a straight hitter it was as rare a prospect as the sight of Davis heading for the tenth fairway was a familiar one, and as such worthy of comment.

"What are you doing over here, George?" he asked pleasantly, as Fidler drew near. "You're usually straight down the middle."

"Bollocks," said Fidler.

Meanwhile Jenkins, on arriving at his ball on the right-hand side of the fairway, noticed another ball about ten yards to his right, in the edge of the light rough. He raised an arm and beckoned to Fidler. "I think this must be your ball over here, George."

As Fidler made his way over Jenkins stepped over to the ball to identify it. Having done so he called out to Fidler again. "Sorry George, false alarm, it can't be yours, it's a Pinnacle and you always play Top Flight fours, don't you."

"Bollocks," said Fidler.

Jenkins blinked. "I beg your pardon?"

Fidler marched up to him and stopped no more than six inches away, red-faced, hands clenched and barely able to contain his rage. "Are you taking the piss?"

Jenkins backed away. "Taking the.....? No, of course not. What do you mean?"

Fidler stepped back a little to give himself room to wag a threatening finger under Jenkins' nose. "Just watch it that's all!" he barked, and with that stepped into the light rough and took a vicious swipe at his ball, sending it back in the general direction of the tenth fairway. He set off after it but before he had taken two steps there was the sound of the ball hitting a tree.

"Shit!" said Fidler.

Jenkins watched him go, then called to Venables. "I wonder why George has changed from Top Flight after all these years."

"And into an arsehole," said Venables.

—⁘—

On the second hole Bramwell had hit his tee shot to the right side of the fairway whilst both Plumstone and Healey were up the left side. Plumstone, watched by Healey, now played his approach shot to the green. He made a complete hash of it, topping it, the ball squirting along the ground some thirty yards before coming to a stop.

"A Daphne Bramwell," said Healey.

"What's that?" said Plumstone.

"Even uglier than Sally Gunnell and not even a good runner."

—◊◊◊—

Jones-Jones was having second thoughts about adopting Cuddington's new way of swinging a golf club as advised by the pro at the Municipal. Not because Cuddington wasn't having any success with it, on the contrary it was working very well indeed, but because Treforest had tried it with his drive off the second tee and had come unstuck. Whether Treforest's club foot was influential in it, or whether the problem was that he had made fewer mistakes coming down than he had made going back or fewer mistakes going back than he had coming down wasn't clear, but what was clear was that when coming down he had made a complete dog's breakfast of it and instead of hitting the ball had hit his good foot. The blow was quite a severe one as the new swing, although failing him miserably, had generated quite a bit of extra clubhead speed. His foot had immediately begun to swell up and throb painfully, which had caused him to walk with a limp. As his wearing of a special boot with a three inch thick sole to cater for his club foot meant that he already walked with a limp he was now limping with both feet, which had the effect of making him look as though he was walking normally, albeit hobbling a bit.

Treforest was pleased about this in a way, as he'd never walked without a limp before, but not so pleased that the price of his improved locomotion was a very sore foot, so when the pain eventually subsided over the course of the next few holes and he started limping normally again he didn't make a further attempt at the new swing for fear of getting the same result.

The record at Sunnymere for ripping up one's card and taking no further part in the competition stood at one hole played. It was jointly held by James Miller Snr, and set in 1969 when it dawned on him as he was about to tee off at the second that in his haste to get to the course on time on his return home from a holiday in Cornwall to take part in the Club Championship he had inadvertently left his wife and children at a motorway services station south of Chesterfield. Miller shared the record with Edward 'Bunty' Bunting, who in 1963 took no further part in the July Monthly Medal after reaching the first green, and on discovering he had holed his two hundred and thirty yard approach shot had suffered a terminal heart attack brought on by the excitement of this achievement. These long-standing records were soon to be broken in terms of holes completed, though not in time taken, by Alan Hartley.

Hartley was a man who liked to get on with the game with the minimum of fuss and delay, and didn't mind who knew it. In fact he took great pains to make sure everyone did know it, working on the principle that the greater the number of members who knew about his abhorrence of slow play the more likely it would be that the ones who chose to play golf at a more leisurely pace would avoid playing with him and risk incurring his wrath.

Not that Hartley ever gave them much opportunity. In friendly fourballs he always ensured that he played with golfers who he knew would try to play the game in the manner he himself did, and avoided like the plague those who didn't. And in competitions, not wishing a slow player to put down his name alongside his own, he would always let the entry sheet fill up a little before adding his own name to the names of two golfers who he knew played the game with reasonable dispatch. He wasn't always able to manage this and sometimes the only spaces available were alongside those golfers he knew to be slow players. On these occasions Hartley would choose not to enter the competition rather than play with them. Absolute anathema to Hartley was to be placed in the position whereby he was forced to let the group behind him play through. He would far rather chew his leg off.

For the Captain's Day competition Hartley had put his name down alongside the names of Neil Critchlow and Paul Collis, two golfers he had played with on numerous occasions, both of whom liked to get on with the game. However at the last minute Collis had withdrawn when his wife had gone into labour – although why this should prevent him from playing his round of golf Hartley was at a loss to explain, as would a fair number of the male members at Sunnymere - and his place had been taken by Peter Moss.

Hartley had played with Moss once before and that single occasion had been enough to last him a lifetime, in fact it had seemed to him as if it had lasted a lifetime, and if he had known about the change in advance he would certainly have withdrawn from the competition. However he had no inkling of the substitution until Moss arrived on the first tee all merry and bright at the appointed time, so he had little alternative but to grin and bear it.

He grinned and bore it for all of three minutes, during which time they had all teed off, set off up the fairway together, and Hartley had discovered that after a distance of less than fifty yards Moss had already dropped fifteen yards behind. He called to him in a voice that he hoped sounded long-suffering as well as business-like, so that perhaps its tone as well as his words might speed up his playing partner a little, "Do try to keep up would you, Peter."

"What's the rush?" said Moss. Then, two dawdling paces on, he suddenly stopped dead in his tracks, cupped a hand to his ear and said, "I say, isn't that a willow warbler?"

The bird in question could have been a wandering albatross or a marsh harrier for all Hartley knew but he said, "Yes, can't be anything else, I'd recognise one a mile off; now get a move on will you, there's a good chap." He waited for Moss to catch up, which Moss commenced to do only after a few more blissful moments listening to the cascading song of the willow warbler. While Hartley waited for Moss to catch up, keeping a beady eye on him in case he should stop again to identify a death watch beetle on the fairway or spot an Australian bush whippet in the rough, he remembered that in addition to Moss's slow play there was something else he didn't like about the man. However he couldn't for the moment recall what it was.

—w—

On the eighth hole Stock's ball had landed in the first of the two bunkers on the right hand side of the fairway. When he arrived at the hazard Stock found that his ball wasn't lying too badly and he was in no doubt that he would be able to get it out; however it was a little too close to the front of the bunker for comfort and he was aware that if he was a bit too greedy and tried to get too much distance on the stroke, and didn't make perfect contact, he could very well end up in the second of the bunkers, which was strategically situated twenty yards further up the fairway.

Armitage and Grover, no strangers to bunkers themselves, and mindful of what would be going through Stock's mind, waited respectfully whilst he made up his mind which type of bunker shot to play. If it had been up to Grover he wouldn't have had any doubts about it; as the ball was sitting up quite nicely he would have taken a nine iron as opposed to a sand wedge, and rather than try to explode the ball out of the bunker would have tried to nip it cleanly off the top of the sand and settle for advancing it seventy yards or so up the fairway, with a bit of luck. If it had been Armitage's shot the decision would have been much more difficult to make, as not only would he have been faced with the choice of which type of shot to play, but having made that decision he would then have to choose which ball to hit, as due to the hallucinatory effect of the space cakes he could now see four balls, two with each of his two heads, two of the balls being a bright pink colour, the other two in a fetching shade of duck egg blue.

Stock finally made up his mind, choosing to blast the ball out onto the middle of the fairway rather than go for distance, took his sand wedge from his bag and stepped with perfectly warranted trepidation into the bunker. There, having given the proposed recovery shot the preparation and concentration it demanded and taken up his stance, he was about to execute it when the helicopter, not for the first time that morning, passed low overhead across his eye line. Stock frowned at it, straightened up from his address position and waited for it to disappear from view. Then he said to the others, "I hope I've seen the last of that bloody chopper."

"As the actress said to the bishop," said Armitage.

Grover grimaced. "Oh for God's sake give it a rest will you Trevor. You've got dicks on the brain, you really have."

—⁓—

By the time Hartley had drawn level with Moss's drive, some two hundred yards or so down the left side of the fairway, Moss himself had fallen about sixty yards behind, due to his having stopped twice, once to identify a rare grasshopper and once to admire a skein of wild geese high overhead, which he watched until it disappeared from view behind the tops of the trees bordering the third fairway. When he arrived at his ball Hartley was waiting for him impatiently with hands on hips. "You really will have to get a move on you know Peter," he admonished him. "If we're not careful the threesome behind us will be calling for us to let them through."

"Oh I doubt that," said Moss, and in a leisurely fashion began to weigh up the distance to the green in preparation for his approach shot.

"Well I don't doubt it for one moment," warned Hartley. "So just try to play with a little more urgency, would you."

Moss regarded Hartley for a moment or so, then reflected, "I think it was Walter Hagen who once remarked that when you're playing a round of golf you should take time to smell the flowers."

"What?" said Hartley.

"You should take time to smell the flowers. When playing golf."

Hartley's patience was finally exhausted. He glared at Moss. "Time to smell the flowers? Time to smell the flowers? You take enough time to grow the fucking flowers. Now get a move on for God's sake. Unless of course you've got any more gems of wisdom up your sleeve?" he added, sarcastically.

"Well there is Sir Walter Simpson's observation," said Moss, and went on to quote the author of The Art of Golf. "'Golf is not one of those occupations in which you soon learn your level. There is no shape nor size of the body, no awkwardness or ungainliness, which puts good golf beyond one's reach. There are good golfers with spectacles, with one eye, with one leg, even with one arm. None but the absolutely blind need despair. It is not the youthful tyro alone who has cause to hope. Beginners in the middle age have become great, and, more wonderful still, after years of patient duffering, there may be a rift in the clouds. Some pet vice which has been clung to as virtue may be abandoned, and the fifth-class player burst upon the world as a medal winner. In golf, whilst there is life there is hope.'"

Hartley glared at Moss. "Have you quite finished?" he asked. A grave mistake, brought about by his having failed to observe, the last time he'd tried it, that sarcasm was a ploy that was completely wasted on Moss.

Moss thought for a moment then set off again. "'Wherein do the charms of this game lie, that captivate youth, and retain their hold still far on in life? It is a fine, open-air, athletic exercise, not violent, but bringing into play nearly all the muscles in the body; while that exercise can be continued for hours....'"

It was at this point that Hartley remembered the other thing he didn't like about Moss. The man was a walking anthology of golf; not only that, he was liable to quote from his reservoir of quotations at the drop of a hat. Hartley quickly picked up the hat he had metaphorically dropped and said, "Yes, yes, all right, I get the point, now can we get on? Please?"

However Moss was in full flight by now, and unstoppable. He continued, "....'It is a game of skill, needing mind and thought and judgement, as well as a cunning hand. It is also a social game, where one may go out with one friend or with three, as the case may be, and enjoy mutual intercourse, mingled with an excitement which is very pleasing. It never palls or grows stale, as morning by morning the players appear at the teeing ground with as keen a relish as if they had not seen a club for a month. Nor is it only while the game lasts that its zest is felt. How the player loves to recall the strokes and other incidents of the match, so that it is often played over again next morning while still in bed' - James Balfour, 1887."

"Fore!" came a loud cry from behind them. Hartley and Moss turned to see the distant figures on the first tee waving at them to get out of the way.

"I think we'd better let them through," said Moss. "I don't like to be pressed."

—⚬—

Southfield was in bed enjoying a post-coital cigarette and contemplating a second carnal encounter with his lover Jessica in the not too distant future. They might do it stood up in the shower, he always enjoyed that, or then again he might let her be the dominant partner for a change, it had been a few weeks since he'd had a spanking, which is what usually happened as a prelude to the sex act whenever he let her take charge of proceedings. Or perhaps he'd simply settle for the good old-fashioned missionary position, a method he never tired off, as contrary to the saying 'You don't look at the mantelpiece when you're poking the fire' he loved to look at Jessica's lovely mantelpiece while he was poking her. Or maybe she could dress up as someone again? With perhaps a 69 for starters, although the last time he'd suggested one she'd turned him down as the time before that she'd taken umbrage when he remarked that the 69 they'd just had was very nice but not as good as the 69 he'd shot at Lindrick the previous week on a day out with the Probus Club. But he was sure he'd be able to talk her round. He sighed contentedly; what a wonderful dilemma to be in.

Jessica was standing at the bedroom window looking out. Something now attracted her attention. She turned to Southfield and beckoned to him. "Quick, come here."

"I'd rather come here again," said Southfield, not a man to turn down the chance to enrich a conversation with a double entendre whenever the opportunity presented itself.

Jessica ignored the quip. "I can see him," she said, nodding in the direction of the golf course beyond the window. "Walking up the fairway. Come and have a look."

It wasn't perhaps the last thing Southfield would have contemplated doing, but would have been well in the running. It was bad enough Jessica standing at the window on her own, never mind standing there with him looking over her shoulder. Even Jessica standing at the window on her own worried him as he had visions of her husband spotting her, wondering what on earth she was doing in the bedroom at this time of the morning, and rushing home to investigate; which would lead no doubt to his being on the wrong end of a thrashing. "Come away from the window," he urged her. "Before the bugger sees you."

Jessica shrugged. "So what if he does see me? I'm only looking out of the window; where's the harm in that?"

Southfield felt she had omitted a relevant point from her assessment of the current situation and now pointed it out. "You haven't got a bloody stitch on Jessica."

"Well I always sleep in the nude, he knows that. He'll think I've just got up. Well he would if he happened to look up and see me, but he won't, he'll be too wrapped up in his stupid game of golf to notice anything."

Southfield knew she had a point. Once a man is out on the golf course he has little thought for anything else;

he was the same himself. And was precisely the reason why he was at this very moment in Jessica's bed contemplating a second bout of sex with her, secure in the knowledge that he was quite safe from discovery whilst doing so, he assured himself.

—⚡—

"Mark McCard."
"Jay Cloth."
"E Gil Three."

—⚡—

Arbuthnott, still holding his game together very well and with an exceptional card in prospect, better even than the net sixty two Alec Adams had decided he would put in, stepped onto the thirteenth tee. He looked down towards the green from its elevated position to establish where they had placed the flagstick that day, expecting to see a difficult pin placement in view of the Nearest the Pin competition taking place there. What he didn't expect to see was a party of three ladies seated behind the green under the shade of a large pink and white candy-striped parasol taking morning coffee. He turned to Bagley and Chapman in disbelief. "I don't believe this!"

"What's that?" said Bagley, as he and Chapman joined Arbuthnott on the tee.

Arbuthnott pointed towards the green.

"Jesus wept!" said Chapman. "I thought I'd seen everything the time one of them discovered a fairy ring in the middle of the twelfth fairway and cordoned it off with pink ribbon."

"They're from the Planet Gladys, women golfers, aren't they," said Bagley, shaking his head in disbelief.

"Well at least they aren't sitting in front of the green," said Arbuthnott, "That's something to be grateful for. I wouldn't put that past them."

"I'd like to put the contents of a double-barrelled shotgun past them," said Chapman, wistfully. "Or better still into them."

128

Behind the green Mrs Quayle, Mrs Rattray and Mrs Salinas had failed to spot the arrival of Arbuthnott, Bagley and Chapman on the tee, their minds occupied with more important matters.

"And the mess they made!" said Mrs Quayle.

Mrs Rattray commiserated with her friend. "Oh it was the same when I had my conservatory installed. The dust got simply everywhere."

"And they don't care," said Mrs Salinas.

"They simply could not care less," agreed Mrs Rattray.

"To be quite honest with you," said Mrs Quayle, "I almost wished we'd never gone in for one in the first place. The whole experience was quite traumatic."

"Well of course having a conservatory installed can be," said Mrs Rattray. "Well no one knows that more than I do."

"Well it's over with now, Miriam," Mrs Salinas consoled her.

"And thank goodness, I don't think I could have stood another day of it."

There was a sudden 'plop' as Arbuthnott's ball landed in the sand bunker to their left.

"Ah," said Mrs Rattray, hearing the sound and noticing the distant figures on the tee, "Our first customers. Now who has the tape measure?"

Back on the tee Arbuthnott bemoaned his luck on seeing his ball land in the bunker. "Shit! That's the first really bad shot I've hit all day. I've those bloody women to thank for that!"

"I'll see if I can hit them for you," said Bagley, taking Arbuthnott's place on the tee.

"Aim for the whites of their eyes," advised Chapman, then had an afterthought. "Make that the whites of their thighs, it's a bigger target."

—⁓—

It had taken less than half-an-hour for Millicent to locate her father. Mr Harkness played bowls in the park most mornings when the weather was fit and today found him there as usual. Persuading him to abandon his game of bowls had been easy as he was losing at the time and the winner paid for the teas; and once Millicent had mentioned that a free drink was involved she had no trouble in talking two of his fellow bowlers into joining him.

On arriving back at the beer tent Millicent was glad to note that the gin level in the bottle of Gordon's hadn't gone down any further. She would have been less glad had she known that in her absence the Lady Captain had helped herself to a couple of generous measures and brought the level back up with water. This of course had the effect of weakening the brew, which was not of course an ideal state of affairs for the Lady Captain, who would have preferred it stronger rather than weaker, but she planned to accidentally break the bottle shortly, which would necessitate opening a new one.

Millicent introduced the three old men to the Lady Captain. "This is my father, Mr Harkness, and these are two of his friends, Mr Oldknow and Mr Wormald. They will be having a drink with us when the Lord Mayor arrives."

"When the Mayor arrives?" said Wormald. "You didn't say anything about having to wait until the Mayor arrives, I want one now, I'm thirsty."

"I want mine now, too," said Oldknow. "Or else I'm going."

"Very well," said Millicent, against her better judgement. She turned to the Lady Captain. "Father will have a small orange juice. I don't know what Mr Oldknow and Mr Wormald would like, very probably the same."

"A pint of bitter," said Oldknow.

"Make that two," said Wormald.

Millicent would have far rather Oldknow and Wormald kept to soft drinks, preferably small ones, being all too aware of what old men were like with their bladders after drinking pints of beer, and had visions of the two of them being otherwise engaged in the lavatory instead of on duty in the beer tent during the Mayoral visit, thus defeating the object of the exercise, but accepted there was little she could do about it. Other than to ensure that they only had one pint of beer each and not a drop more, which she fully intended to do.

—⁓—

All three tee shots at the thirteenth had failed to find the green. Arbuthnott's ball in the bunker was the nearest to the pin, Bagley was left and short whilst Chapman was even shorter and right.

As the three golfers were approaching their respective balls Mrs Quayle, Mrs Rattray and Mrs Salinas, the latter now armed with a tape measure, left their chairs and ambled onto the green in the direction of the bunker in which Arbuthnott's ball had landed. Mrs Quayle called to them, gaily. "Good morning, gentlemen. We'll try not to hold you up for too long."

"What?" said Chapman. "What do you think you're doing?"

"Measuring the nearest ball to the pin of course," said Mrs Salinas, brightly.

"Measuring the nearest ball to the pin?" echoed Bagley, just as surprised as Chapman had been.

"We have to measure the nearest ball to the pin," exclaimed Mrs Rattray, patiently. "Didn't you know? Mr Arbuthnott's ball I believe."

"But why?" said Chapman. "It isn't going to win."

"It might," said Mrs Salinas.

Arbuthnott turned to Bagley. "You're right, Baggers. The Planet Gladys."

"What's the matter?" asked Mrs Salinas of Arbuthnott, detecting the tone of ridicule in his voice without at all understanding what he'd meant.

"Well I'm twenty yards from the pin in a bunker, aren't I," explained Arbuthnott. "How can I possibly win a Nearest the Pin Competition?"

"Well the lady who won our Nearest the Pin Competition was twenty seven yards and four inches away from the pin," said Mrs Quayle, "So you must be in with some sort of a chance."

"Twenty seven yards and four inches?" echoed Arbuthnott, then added, sarcastically, "Was it on the green?"

"There's nothing in the competition rules that says it has to be on the green," said Mrs Rattray, authoritatively.

"It wasn't even on the green?"

"It was in a bunker if you must know. That one over there." She pointed to another bunker. "Front edge."

Arbuthnott was quickly running out of patience. "Look get off the green, will you, I've got a good round going," he said, then modified his claim. "Well I did have a good round going until I saw you lot having a bloody tea party."

"And what is that supposed to mean?" demanded Mrs Quayle.

"Look, just clear off out of it will you!" said Chapman.

Mrs Rattray leapt to her friend's defence. "You can't talk to Mrs Quayle like that. She's just had a conservatory in!"

"I couldn't give a shit if she's just had the milkman in, clear off," said Chapman.

"Well!" said Mrs Quayle. "If that doesn't take the biscuit! Mr Captain will hear of this."

—◊—

In Daddy Rhythm's considered opinion Millicent had been far too dismissive about Lord Nose and the Bogies and he felt that once she'd had the chance to hear them she would very quickly become a fan. With his equipment finally set up the disc-jockey was now about to put this theory to the test. Initially his plan had been to wait until the dinner dance to surprise Millicent and the rest of the golf club with the talents of his favourite group, but then changed his mind and decided that if he were to give everyone a preview of the delights to come it would cheer them up a bit if their golf wasn't going too well, in addition to giving them all something to look forward to.

One of the giant loudspeakers was already pointing in the direction of the large windows that looked out onto the golf course and Daddy Rhythm now muscled the other one round until it was pointing the same way as its twin. He had already opened wide all the windows. Now he cued in the second track of the CD 'Lord Nose and the Bogies Greatest Tits', cranked up the volume of the three amplifiers to maximum, and seconds later a hundred and twenty decibels of 'I Don't Give a Toss', but sounding even louder due to the screech of Lord Nose's falsetto voice and drummer Snot Green's generous use of his two base drums and crash cymbals, hit the golf course.

> I don't give a toss
> You could be nailed to a cross
> But it's sod all to do with me
> 'cos I don't give a toss
> I'm like Jonathan Woss
> And I don't give a toss toss toss!

> I don't give a shite
> You might think that's not right
> But it's sod all to do with you
> 'cos I don't give a shite
> As long as I'm all right
> No I don't give a shite shite shite!

> I don't give a fuck
> So you're down on your luck
> Well it's sod all to do with me
> 'cos I don't give a fuck
> So that's your fucking luck
> For I don't give a fuck fuck fuck!

The pro's shop was situated between the clubhouse and the golf course and received the full blast of it.

"Awesome," said Darren.

—⚬—

The sound was almost as loud in the beer tent where, along with everyone else within a mile, Millicent learned that Lord Nose and the Bogies didn't give a toss and didn't give a shite. However, unlike everyone else, she never did find out they didn't give a fuck as just before the start of the third verse she fainted.

"You'd better move her outside," advised the Lady Captain to Millicent's father and his friends as soon as the song had ended and she could hear herself speak, "where she can get some fresh air."

—◊—

Mr Captain was returning from the beer tent when the fusillade of S, W and F-words hit him, a phenomenon that had rendered him absolutely mortified and had made a very large contribution towards his day being spoiled. His mortification however was tempered by the relief that it hadn't happened in the presence of the Lord Mayor. He now made for the clubhouse and Daddy Rhythm to ensure that that terrible prospect could never come about.

10.40 a.m.
R Thompson (12)
R Livermore (17)
J Purseglove (18)

After Moss had signalled the threesome behind to play through, Ray Livermore hit his tee shot into the left-hand rough and it took he and his playing partners Reg Thompson and John Purseglove about three minutes to find it. After Livermore had whacked the wayward ball some fifty yards or so back onto the fairway and they had all set off after it Thompson said: "So this Englishman pitched up in this little village in the middle of Wales and the place was deserted except for this old Welshman sat on a bench at the side of the road, and the Englishman said to him 'Excuse me, I'm looking for a man called Evans. We met on holiday at Butlin's recently; you wouldn't happen to know where he lives, would you?' And the Welshman said 'Well we've got a lot of people called Evans in this village, boyo, it's a very popular name in these parts is Evans, we have more people called Evans than we have called Jones and we have a lot of people called Jones. Can you tell me anything about him?' And the Englishman said 'He has very blonde hair.' And the Welshman said 'It could be Evans the Butcher then, he has very blonde hair. Is he tall?' And the Englishman said 'No he's quite short actually.' And the Welshman said 'Very blonde and quite short, eh? That sounds like Evans the Baker, he's blonde and quite short. Is he fat?' And the Englishman said 'No, he's quite thin.' And the Welshman said 'Very blonde, quite short and quite thin, eh? That sounds like Evans the Grocer. Did he walk with a limp?' And the Englishman said 'No, he walked perfectly normally.' And the Welshman said 'Not him either then. Can you tell me anything else about him?' And the Englishman said 'Well like I said we met on holiday at Butlin's, he was in the next chalet to us and we got quite friendly, then on the last day of the holiday while I was out he had sex with my wife, then stole my best suit out of the wardrobe with my wallet and all my money in it, then to top it off he shit on my doorstep.' And the Welshman said 'Oh you mean Evans the Twat.'"

Livermore and Purseglove burst out laughing.

"Wonderful," said Livermore.

"A cracker," agreed Purseglove.

By then they were almost upon Hartley, Critchlow and Moss who were waiting at the side of the fairway. Hartley was absolutely seething. He glared at them and said, "So it's something to laugh about is it? Us having to let you through?"

"No," said Purseglove.

"Not at all," said Livermore.

"Then why are you laughing?"

"Reg just told us a very funny joke," said Purseglove.

"Oh I like a good joke," said Moss, his face lighting up, "Tell it to us would you Reg?"

Thompson took a deep breath. "Well this Englishman pitched up in this little village in the middle of Wales, and the place..."

Hartley went ballistic. "Do you bloody mind?" he snarled, steam coming from his ears. "We're trying to play a game of golf here!"

"Steady on Alan," said Livermore, noting the veins standing out on Hartley's forehead, "you'll be doing yourself a mischief."

Moss now saw the opportunity for another cautionary tale from his treasury of golf anecdotes and seized on it like a hungry ferret that had waylaid a careless rabbit. He started to recite: "As Dr A S Lamb once said, 'Golf increases the blood pressure, ruins the disposition, induces neurasthenia, hurts...'"

That was as far as he got, and if Critchlow hadn't had the presence of mind to dive in and grab Hartley in a bear hug when the latter drew back his arm to smite Moss on the jaw Hartley would now be an ex-member of Sunnymere (golf clubs not taking kindly to members hitting each other, except with golf balls of course, which is unavoidable given the nature of the game and the skills of those participating in it). In the event Critchlow's intervention, although not making Hartley any less angry with Moss, at least slowed him down enough for him to contemplate what might be the possible outcome should he succeed in carrying out the assault on his playing partner. Common sense prevailed after a few moments and Hartley visibly calmed down. Critchlow released him, whereupon Hartley, not trusting himself to say another word, grabbed hold of his trolley and marched back down the fairway and off the course. He had played just two hundred and thirty yards of the first of the eighteen holes. A new record.

—ᗰ—

On his way to deal in no uncertain terms with Daddy Rhythm Mr Captain was surprised by the sight of two police constables accompanied by a small boy making their way on to the golf course. Mr Captain's hackles rose immediately. Sunnymere Golf Club was private property and could be visited only at the invitation of a member, and he was quite certain that no one would have offered an invitation to two uniformed policemen and a scruffy little boy, and especially on Captain's Day. He waited until they were almost level with him then stepped in front of them and said, "Yes, can I help you?" in a tone of voice which made it quite clear that it would be highly unlikely he would be able to help anyone who had obviously no right to be there in the first place.

Constable Fearon did not like golf. As a sport he rated it somewhere between topless darts and synchronized tiddlywinks. A dyed-in-the-wool Labour Party supporter of the old school he had always held the opinion that golf was a class-ridden game and that those who played it were fancy-trousered dickheads, and had once expressed the opinion that if golfers were to appear in the street in the same clothes in which they paraded themselves on the golf course they would be locked up, and he would like to be the one who did the locking up.

If he had little time for golfers he had even less time for golfers who had recently abused his son by tying him to a golf trolley with a pair of shoelaces and had then proceeded to cart him round the golf course for a few holes, and about the same amount of time for ones dressed in plus fours and stupid tartan hats like the one confronting him at the moment.

Furthermore he was far better at detecting irony than he would ever be at detecting crime, and Mr Captain's condescending 'Yes, can I help you?' had done nothing to improve his opinion of golfers, and was the reason he now gave him even shorter shrift than he would normally have given to a golfer. "Out of the bleeding way Severiano," he snarled, pushing Mr Captain aside.

Mr Captain was a law abiding citizen; however the constables were on the golf course, his golf course, of which he was the captain, and if anyone was going anywhere, policemen or no policemen, he would know the reason why. "And what is the purpose of your visit?" he demanded, tracking back and getting himself in front of Constable Fearon again and barring his way.

Fearon stopped and regarded Mr Captain as though he were a petty criminal he had just apprehended whilst trying to mug an old lady. "Not that it's any of your business but my child has reported to me that one of your golfers has abused him," he said, indicating Jason, who was clearly enjoying the confrontation.

"One of our golfers?" Mr Captain shook his head violently. "Quite impossible. When is this unlikely scenario supposed to have happened?"

"It isn't *supposed* to have happened, it did happen. Earlier this morning. He tied him to his golf trolley."

"Tied him to his golf trolley?" Mr Captain shook his head again. "A golfer would never do that. Especially not a Sunnymere member. There must be some mistake."

"Yes and the bent bastard who tied my boy to his trolley has made it. Show him your wrists, Jason."

Jason did as he was bidden. "They're all red see." he said, pointing to the weals on his wrists. "Where the shoelaces dug in."

Mr Captain glanced at Jason's wrists. "He probably did that to himself."

"I'll do you myself if you don't stop giving me lip and start co-operating," said Fearon. "So who's responsible for it?"

"They called him Mr Vice, Dad." said Jason. "The one who did it."

Fearon's face lit up. "Mr Vice? Why didn't you tell me that before?"

"I've only just remembered."

Fearon scratched his chin. "Mr Vice, eh? So it would appear we could have a *sexually-motivated* crime on our hands."

Mr Captain didn't care at all for the way the conversation was heading and now nipped in smartly to stop it heading any farther in that direction. "No, you misunderstand completely. Mr Vice isn't his real name. His real name is Robin Garland."

Fearon leapt onto this new development immediately. "So Mr Vice is an alias?"

"What? No, he's just known as Mr Vice by the members."

"Why? What's he into this Mr Vice character? Sado-masochism I shouldn't wonder, tying little boys up."

"Or he could be a paedophile," said Constable James, now joining in the conversation, paedophile crimes being a speciality of his, as well as his hobby. "Sounds to me like he's a paedophile, Fearo."

"He isn't anything of the sort," protested Mr Captain. "He's a perfectly respectable gentleman."

"That's the impression they all give," said Fearon, knowledgeably. "It's a front; butter wouldn't melt with some of the bastards. But what respectable man goes about tying kids up? Eh? Now get out of my way before I do you for obstructing a police officer in the course of his duty."

Mr Captain was not prepared to give up the battle just yet however. He now played his trump card. "I'm afraid it is quite impossible for you to go onto the golf course."

"What?"

"You simply aren't allowed to. You're not a member."

Fearon fixed Mr Captain with a baleful stare. "A crime has been committed. In the pursuit of bringing the perpetrator of that crime to justice I can go anywhere I like. Understand?"

Mr Captain knew there was no argument with Fearon's contention so had no alternative but to beg. "But …look…..I mean it's Captain's Day," he said, plaintively.

"What?"

"It's Captain's Day. And I'm the Captain."

"I couldn't give a shit if it's the Admiral of the fucking Fleet's day and you're Lord fucking Nelson, me and Constable James are going on that golf course and arresting the sado-masochist paedophile bastard who abused my son," said Fearon, jabbing his finger into Mr Captain's chest with every third or fourth word, and every single word of 'sado-masochist paedophile bastard'. "Got that, sunshine?"

Mr Captain had. And knew there wasn't a lot he could do about it. He just hoped it wouldn't spoil his day too much.

—⁓—

The reaction of Hanson and Galloway on seeing Mrs Quayle, Mrs Rattray and Mrs Salinas taking morning coffee behind the thirteenth green was similar to that of the Arbuthnott threesome a few minutes earlier.

"Look at them," scoffed Hanson, forgetting all his illnesses for a moment. "Have you ever seen anything like it in your life?"

"Not outside a nuthouse," said Galloway.

Irwin was considerably more hostile than his playing partners about the situation which confronted them. "If I hit a bad shot through being put off by those old boilers," he said, "I am going to take my putter and ram it up their arses."

"That's what my anal pain feels like, somebody shoving a putter up my bum," said Hanson, Irwin's words reminding him of one of his illnesses. "And did I mention my lumbago had come back?"

—⁓—

"Divot Large."
"Dodd G Swing."
"Shank Sallot."

—⁓—

"Breast augmentation?" said Mrs Salinas, as Hanson's ball joined Galloway's on the green.

"Well that's what she said she wanted," said Mrs Rattray. "Some people are never satisfied, are they."

"I'm not sure how I feel about that sort of thing," said Mrs Salinas. "Well to tell the truth it's not something I've ever had to consider. I've always been quite content with my breasts."

"Well that goes for me too," said Mrs Rattray, then counselled the opinion of Mrs Quayle. "How do you feel about breast augmentation, Miriam?"

"Oh it's not for me," said Mrs Quayle, not even having to consider the question. "No, I've always been quite happy with just the two."

At that Mrs Salinas shrieked with laughter. Mrs Rattray joined in, equally enthusiastically.

"Two's company, three's a crowd, as the saying goes," Mrs Quayle went on gaily, causing Mrs Salinas to shriek out again.

On the thirteenth tee Irwin, having just reached the top of his backswing when Mrs Salinas's first shriek broke the silence, just managed to pull out of his downswing at the cost of staggering forward a couple of steps and falling off the end of the tee. Absolutely livid, he got to his feet, brandished his club at the ladies and screeched "Bloody splitarses!" Then, as the laughter down on the green didn't show any signs of subsiding, he got back on the tee and bellowed "Fore!" at the top of his voice.

"What's the matter with him?" said Mrs Rattray, looking up at the tee in response to Irwin's shout.

"We're not in his way," said Mrs Salinas. "So why on earth is he shouting fore?"

Mrs Quayle shielded her eyes against the sun as she peered towards the tee. A moment later she recognised

Irwin and pulled a face. "I do believe it's that *man*," she said distastefully.

"What man?" said Mrs Salinas.

"What's his name? That *man*. You know, the one who was asleep on the bench behind the seventh tee on Ladies Day last year, snoring his head off. And when I poked him with my putter to wake him up he swore at me."

"Oh, *that* man," said Mrs Rattray.

—◊◊◊—

Armitage knew what the expression going on a trip meant but not having tried drugs previously the only trips he had ever been on were ones that went to the seaside or the Lake District. Even though one of these trips had included a trip to Morecambe and another a trip to Skegness on a wet Wednesday none of them had been anything nearly so bad as the trip he was experiencing at the moment, not even the pub trip to Blackpool from the Pan and Kettle when he and three friends had had far too much to drink in the Tower Bar and had gone roller-skating in Olympia and he'd ended up shitting in his trousers and vomiting over a couple from Accrington.

The double vision had gone, thankfully, after he had hit on the idea of closing one eye, and had worked quite well until, robbed of peripheral vision to his left, he had walked into a tree and cracked his head.

It had been replaced by fear. A terrible, all encompassing, abject fear. He couldn't for the life of him have told you what he was frightened about, only that it wasn't the fear of the unknown, or indeed of the known, but a fear ten times more frightening than both of them put together, and that if only it had gone away he would gladly have put up with seeing double or walking into trees and cracking his head or shitting in his trousers and vomiting over couples from Accrington every day for the rest of his life.

—◊◊◊—

When Irwin had eventually taken his tee shot his ball had landed on the green and come to rest no more than six feet

142

from the flagstick. Mrs Quayle, Mrs Rattray and Mrs Salinas had looked at the ball on the green, then at each other. Each of the ladies knew instinctively what had to be done. Mrs Quayle was the first to put their thoughts into words. "Well *he* certainly isn't going to win the Nearest the Pin competition."

"He most certainly is not," agreed Mrs Rattray.

"Not in the proverbial month of Sundays," said Mrs Salinas.

The matter settled, Mrs Quayle put down her coffee cup and chocolate digestive, got to her feet, walked purposefully to Irwin's ball and without ceremony kicked it off the green.

"What's known as judicious use of the leather mashie, as they say in the vernacular I believe, ladies," she said, as she made her way back to the folding chair she'd got from John Lewis's.

—◊◊◊—

"So that's one orange juice and two pints of bitter, if I remember rightly?" said the Lady Captain to Mr Harkness, Mr Oldknow and Mr Wormald on their return to the beer tent after they'd deposited Millicent Fridlington round the back of it. "Unless you'd like something a little stronger, now your daughter isn't around, Mr Harkness?" she added, with a knowing wink to Millicent's father.

Millicent safely out of the way for the time being Harkness leapt at the opportunity. "I don't mind if I do, my dear."

"My late husband Bobby used to say that a pint of bitter always went down better when it was accompanied by a chaser," said the Lady Captain, putting a pint glass under the firkin of beer and opening the tap.

"Your late husband Bobby knew what he was talking about," said Oldknow.

"So that will be three whiskies in addition to the three pints of bitter then, gentlemen?"

"Doubles," said Wormald.

—◊◊◊—

The three ladies were waiting on the green with the tape measure as Galloway, Hanson and Irwin approached.

Mrs Quayle gave them a pleasant smile and trilled, "Good morning, gentlemen."

Galloway touched his cap and greeted the measuring party; it didn't cost anything and Mrs Rattray was a near neighbour. "Ladies."

"Lovely day," said Mrs Salinas.

"Well it would be if it wasn't for my neck and my back," agreed Hanson.

"Really?" said Mrs Rattray. "What's the matter with them?"

However before Hanson had chance to regale Mrs Rattray with the latest on his neck and back Irwin realised his ball wasn't on the green.

"Where's my ball?" he asked, puzzled.

"Is that it over there?" said Mrs Quayle, with a display of innocence that would have done credit to a virgin bride, pointing to Irwin's ball in the shallow bunker guarding the front left of the green.

Irwin hit the roof. "It landed right next to the flagstick!"

"That's right," said Mrs Salinas. "It did. Then it set off again. Didn't it, ladies?"

"Like they do," said Mrs Rattray.

"Backspin, I believe," said Mrs Quayle, knowledgeably. "It's you men, you're so powerful. We women can't generate anything like so much backspin, if any at all, can we ladies?" Mrs Salinas and Mrs Rattray concurred. Mrs Quayle went on, "We're so envious of you. And you were quite close to the hole at one stage, Mr Irwin. But *c'est la vie.*" She turned her attention to Galloway and Hanson. "Now I wonder which of you two gentlemen will be taking the early lead?"

"I slightly favour Mr Galloway's ball but it's a close run thing by the look of it," said Mrs Salinas, taking one end of the tape measure and making for Hanson's ball. "We shall have to be extra careful."

"You moved it," accused Irwin, to Mrs Quayle. "You moved my ball!"

"Don't be such a silly-billy," said Mrs Quayle. "Why would I do a thing like that?"

Now that he'd realised what must have happened Irwin dispensed with further chit-chat and cut straight to the chase. "Silly-billy? I'll show you who's a silly-billy, you bloody cow," he said, advancing on Mrs Quayle, arms outstretched in front of him, hands automatically forming neck-sized pincers with which to strangle her.

Mrs Quayle, realising she may have gone too far, began to back away, alarmed. "Stop! What do you think you're doing?" she squealed, as Irwin made a grab for her which she just managed to avoid by jumping smartly backwards. Before he could make another grab for her she pulled herself up to her full height of five feet two inches and commanded, "Don't touch me! Don't you dare touch me, you hear!"

—◌—

In the excitement of dealing with the policemen Mr Captain had forgotten all about Daddy Rhythm and the revolting song he had played for all the world to hear, but now remembering it he strode out for the clubhouse. However when he got there the disc-jockey had left. Mr Captain made a note to deal with the matter prior to the dance commencing that evening, before Daddy Rhythm had the chance to play even so much as a single note of his disgusting music.

G Burton (2)
R Tinson (12)
D Tollemache (16)

Both Dave Tollemache and Graham Burton threw their golf clubs with such regularity that they were known for their club-throwing antics far more than they were for their skill at the game of golf, which in the case of Burton was considerable, in the case of Tollemache less so.

One of Tollemache's claims to fame, though by no means the most unusual one, was that in his disappointment and rage at missing an eighteen inch putt he had once thrown his putter high into the branches of the large oak tree behind the fourth green, whereupon it had become lodged. Despite throwing things at it in an effort to dislodge it, including another club, which had also stopped up there, the putter had steadfastly refused to budge and Tollemache had been forced to continue without it, putting for the remainder of the round with a one iron. This state of affairs had continued until the eighth hole, where he had used the one iron for its correct purpose of driving from the tee, and had hit the ball out of bounds. In his anger Tollemache had flung the one iron even farther out of bounds than he had hit the ball, and although he found the ball after a couple of minutes searching for the club he had less luck in finding the club, and had had to continue his round putting with his two iron. Thankfully the two iron survived all eighteen holes, which is more than can be said for his three wood, which he threw after hitting a very poor drive at the twelfth, the persimmon head of the club parting company with the shaft on smashing into a stone horse trough, persimmon, although devilishly hard, not being anything like so hard as millstone grit.

In 1984 Tollemache had written to the sport's lawmakers, the Royal and Ancient Golf Club of St Andrews, on the subject of the carrying no more than fourteen clubs rule, asking for special dispensation to carry fifteen clubs at the start of his round on the grounds that he either lost or damaged beyond repair at least one of his clubs on the way round, and therefore he needed the extra club to make up his quota at the finish of his round so as not to be at a disadvantage; however that august body wisely turned down his request, obviously fearful of setting a precedent.

Tollemache's record for throwing clubs was nine in one round, and his record distance fifty seven yards with a six iron at the tenth according to his playing partner Simon Pemberton, a chartered surveyor, who had paced out the exact yardage. And he had once brought down a black-headed gull in full flight with a sand wedge, prompting the wittier of his playing partners to comment that it was his first birdie of the day. It wasn't his last, because at the tenth, after ripping up his card and looking for some alternative sport to fill in the time while his partners continued their round, he had thrown another of his clubs at a hovering skylark and bagged it at the third attempt.

It was the first time Tollemache had ever actually aimed at something, all previous club-throwing owing its genesis to anger rather than any desire to hit a target. Encouraged by this early success he took the decision to always aim at something in future, preferably something for the pot, a wood pigeon perhaps, or one of the many rabbits that abounded and bounded on the course, as he was a lover of game and his wife was a dab hand at cooking it. In the event however he was always so angry when he threw a club that he forgot all about his pledge, and the pot remained empty and Mrs Tollemache's culinary skills with game not called upon.

Graham Burton was no less adept nor constant in his club-throwing activities, but although he was not averse to throwing a single club now and again his favoured method of club-throwing was to throw all his clubs at once, usually, but not always, while they were still in his golf bag. On one occasion, on the near-completion of a particularly bad round, he had thrown bag, clubs, golf trolley and all into the large pond by the seventeenth green, before stalking off the course vowing that he would never be seen on the golf course again, and that if somebody did happen to see him on the golf course again they should shoot him. In fact he was seen on it again only five minutes later after he'd realised that his car keys were in his golf bag, and he'd had to wade into the middle of the pond to recover them, the ensuing embarrassment only serving to strengthen his resolve never to return.

However despite his promise it was far from the last time Burton threw his clubs into the pond. No one knew for sure, because records weren't kept until 1992, but since then it had happened eight times. Sometimes they stayed there for upwards of a month, on other occasions for only a couple of days, depending upon how long it took him to realise how much he was missing his golf.

At a touching ceremony in 1998 the pond was officially named Burton's Pond. Burton himself had been due to attend the ceremony and accept a commemorative scroll but in the event had failed to make it as the day before the presentation was due to take place he had thrown his clubs into the pond and given up golf again.

Whenever Burton threw clubs singly, which he tended to do more towards the beginning of a round rather than the end, which was usually the case when he threw the whole bagful, he did not have the range of Tollemache but made up for it by variety, one of his favourite methods being to bend the offending club over his knee before hurling it into the distance like some large metal boomerang, the difference being that it never came back, except on the occasion it hit Sylvester Cuddington on the knee and Cuddington threw it back at him.

In the Captain's Day competition that day neither Tollemache nor Burton had hit good tee shots at the first but neither of their shots had been bad enough to warrant the throwing of a club. However Roy Tinson, the third member of the group, hit a truly awful shot, a shot so bad that had Tollemache or Burton made it their club would most certainly have been flung. However Tinson had never thrown a club in his life so had put his driver back in his bag unflung. Burton and Tollemache marvelled at his temperament.

—ᴍ—

"Perhaps if you were to get your right leg over that branch there Miriam, that knobbly one, and sort of pass it under the branch to the left of it?" suggested Mrs Salinas.

"The nerve of that *man*!" said the deeply upset Mrs Rattray. "He obviously wasn't aware that you are the Lady Captain-Elect, Miriam."

Irwin was a large man and Mrs Quayle a small woman so it had been a relatively easy matter for him to pick her up and deposit her in the branches of the tree. It was proving to be a far from easy matter getting her down again. She had already been up there for ten minutes and despite lots of advice and encouragement from Mrs Rattray and Mrs Salinas she was no nearer to getting down than she had been since the moment Irwin had put her up there, and now had several flesh abrasions caused by her thrashing about in the branches in a vain effort to free herself, to add to her discomfort.

Both Galloway and Hanson had objected most strongly to Irwin's treatment of Mrs Quayle; Galloway because his ball had come to rest no more than eight feet from the hole and he fancied his chances in the Nearest the Pin competition and Mrs Rattray and Mrs Salinas had steadfastly refused to measure the balls so long as Mrs Quayle remained in the tree; Hanson because he would rather Irwin had carried out his threat and shoved his putter up Mrs Quayle's behind so that somebody else would know what it felt like.

Far from happy to relinquish his position as leader in the Nearest the Pin competition Galloway had then suggested to Irwin that he might take Mrs Quayle down from the tree, get the ladies to measure his ball, then put her back up it again. However Irwin, still peeved that he himself would not be the leader, would have none of it, and in the end all three men had putted out without their balls being measured and had continued on to the fourteenth, Galloway somewhat grumpily.

Mrs Salinas now thought she might have the answer to Mrs Quayle's problem. "If you could sort of twist yourself to the right a little, I think…"

"I am quite twisted enough, thank you Elspeth," said Mrs Quayle, with feeling. "Not to mention bitter."

"As would we all be Miriam, as would we all be," said Mrs Salinas, then spat out, "That *man!*"

"There's nothing for it, you will have to get help ladies," said Mrs Quayle. "I can't stay up here for the duration."

"When my cat Montgomery got stuck up a tree the fire brigade got him down," said Mrs Rattray, then added doubtfully, "Although I'm not at all sure if they'd turn out for a lady stuck up a tree."

"Oh I'm sure they would," said Mrs Salinas. "Especially if we told them she was the Lady Captain-Elect."

"I'll phone them," said Mrs Rattray, taking out her mobile phone. "Is it still nine-nine-nine you ring?"

"Oh that's a pretty mobile," said Mrs Rattray. "Such a lovely colour."

"Do you like it? I got it from Marks and Spencer's."

"Debenhams do a nice one in cerise," said Mrs Quayle, from her perch in the tree.

—⁂—

If Mrs Quayle was no nearer to getting down from the tree than when Irwin had put her up there Constable Fearon was even farther away from laying hands on vice-captain Robin Garland than he had been when he'd left Mr Captain at the first tee.

Golf courses cover many acres of land and the problem for Fearon was that he had no idea on which of the many Sunnymere acres Garland was playing his golf at the moment. He had established from Jason that it was the fifth fairway from which he had earlier made good his escape, and that the time of the escape was approximately ten-o-clock. He had no idea how long it took to play a round of golf, only that it seemed to take an eternity from what he'd seen of it on television, nor had Constable James, and nor had Jason, whose only interest in golf was harvesting golf balls for re-sale, so pinpointing Garland's position was proving to be more difficult than he had imagined. Aware that he had to start somewhere Fearon had estimated that each hole took half-an-hour to play, and as Garland had been playing the fifth when Jason escaped and an hour had passed since then, that he should now be playing the seventh. Having established this the three of them set off for the eighth green, the plan being to get ahead of Garland and lie in wait for him.

The first snag they encountered was that none of them knew in which direction the eighth green lay. The problem was exacerbated when Fearon decided to ask one of the golfers for directions and he happened to pick on Venables, a man whose hatred of the police was even greater than Fearon's hatred of golfers, and Venables had sent the party in precisely the opposite direction to that required for safe passage to the eighth green. On arriving at the twelfth, the best part of a mile from where they had set off, and finding it not to be the eighth, James complained that his legs were aching as he wasn't used to walking, and they'd had to rest for ten minutes while he recovered. While they were taking this unscheduled pit stop Jason suggested it might be best if they made their way back to the first tee, then walked each hole just as though they were golfers playing the course, and that this would eventually result in them catching up with Garland as unlike golfers they wouldn't have to keep stopping and looking for balls. Despite having come out top of his class at Police Training College Fearon had been unable to come up with a better idea and they had set off for the first tee.

—⁂—

"Chuck Key."
"Chuck Sillyname."
"Chuck Up."

—⁂—

At the fourteenth Fidler lost the last of the six Pinnacles he had earlier bought from the pro's shop. Abandoning the search he made his way out of the heavy rough, in which he had been looking for the ball with Dawson and Elwes, picked up his golf bag and set off back down the fairway.

"Where are you going?" asked Dawson, puzzled.

Fidler stopped, turned to him. "Well I've run out of balls, haven't I."

"So you're ripping up then?" said Elwes.

"No, I am not ripping up. I am going to the pro's shop to buy some more balls."

"But we're miles away," protested Dawson. "You'll be forever."

"Then you'll just have to wait for me, won't you."

"If you're not back in five minutes we'll continue without you," said Elwes. "You're only allowed five minutes to look for a lost ball, it's in the rules."

"I'm not looking for a lost ball, I'm going shopping for some more; and I'm quite sure there's nothing in the rules that says I can't do that!" said Fidler, adamantly. "And as I'm marking your card you have no alternative but to wait for me until I return," he added, with a smile.

"Play one of your Top Flight fours," said Elwes, in desperation. "You must have some." He reached in the ball pocket of his bag. "I'll mark it for you with my felt tip pen to distinguish it from mine." He cast a glance of warning at Dawson should he upset Fidler any more than he was already upset by suggesting it wouldn't be necessary to mark the ball as Elwes's ball would be on the fairway, as he had previously. However it was too late for conciliatory tactics.

"You can stick your felt tip pen up your arse," said Fidler, and with that strolled off back down the fairway, leaving Dawson and Elwes looking decidedly miffed.

If the playing of 'I Don't Give a Toss' and the arrival of Constables Fearon and James had been influential in spoiling Mr Captain's day to some degree the arrival of Martin Hawker, Peter Simpson and Phyllis Hill at the first tee had the potential to completely ruin it.

Until six months ago Phyllis Hill had been Philip Hill, at which point in his life he had undertaken a sex-change operation. (Armitage, with a possible penis transplant in mind, had enquired as to the size of the unwanted genitalia, but Philip had told him that Phyllis would be holding on to it, figuratively speaking, for sentimental reasons.)

Up until the time of the operation Philip had been a transvestite and when playing golf had dressed as do most lady golfers, in pastel shades and tweedy things, and well-cut trousers, rather than a skirt. Thus attired he could quite easily have been taken for one of the lady members at Sunnymere, not because he looked particularly feminine but because quite a few of the more heftily built lady members could easily be taken for transvestites.

The officials of the club didn't much care for the idea of Philip Hill dressing as a woman but there was very little they could do about it, though it was not for want of trying. The club secretary had scoured the Rules of Golf, and whilst he had found many rules that were complete news to him none of them related to the rights or otherwise of transvestites on the course. And in the politically correct times prevalent in Great Britain in the early years of the third millennium it was of course unthinkable that Philip Hill should be barred from playing his chosen sport just because he chose to dress like a woman. It didn't however stop most of the members from thinking he should. In fact the majority of them would have willingly shot and buried him in the golf course's deepest bunker if they'd thought for one moment they would get away with it.

However the problems posed by having a transvestite on the course were as nothing once Philip had gone through the operation that transformed him into, if not a whole woman, then minus a set of male genitalia a whole woman. For it was then that Philip Hill, now Phyllis Hill, sought to play in the ladies' competitions rather than the men's. Not surprisingly the Sunnymere ladies' section would not even contemplate the proposition. As far as they were concerned Phyllis Hill was still very much a man. That he was a man now minus a penis and testicles, in addition to being the proud owner, thanks to hormone treatment, of a pair of small but blossoming breasts, didn't even enter into the argument. The way the ladies saw it was that although Philip Hill may very well no longer have male genitalia he certainly still did have the same muscular six feet two inch frame he'd had before, as well as the two strong arms of the plasterer's mate he had been (and still was) for the last fifteen years, and therefore had an unfair advantage when it came to propelling a golf ball round the course, and especially so off the ladies' tees.

In an effort to reach some sort of compromise Phyllis had offered to play in the ladies' competitions but off the men's tees, but to no avail. The ladies would not allow her to play in their competitions full stop, and that was the end of the matter. The club chairman George Grover had pointed out to the ladies' committee, as delicately as he could, that Phyllis now had a vagina and bigger breasts than his wife, in fact bigger breasts than quite a number of the lady members, but the ladies had been adamant in their rejection of the new member without a member. Letters had been sent to the R & A and the Ladies Golf Union asking if one or other of those ruling bodies could clarify the situation. Both letters had received no response whatsoever, despite two further letters asking if the original letters had been received, save for a letter postmarked 'St Andrews' from someone with a GSOH requesting a photograph of Phyllis, who he WLTM with a view to a dinner date and possible fun afterwards, non-smoker. Consequently the male membership had had no alternative but to allow Phyllis to continue playing in the men's competitions. For her part Phyllis didn't mind which competitions she played in just so long as she could play.

So it should have been business as usual. However now that Phyllis was a woman, in her eyes if in no one else's, she began to dress more in the manner of what her idea of a woman should dress like. Out went the pastel shades and tweedy things and well-cut trousers; in came much brighter colours and clingy things and skirts. This in itself wouldn't have been too bad, as quite a number of the more adventurous lady members also wore brighter colours, a few of them even wearing clingy things and skirts, but unlike Phyllis they didn't wear a huge pair of falsies under their jumpers - which she had affected until such time as her new breasts reached maturity - and miniskirts, nor the long platinum blonde wig and full make-up Phyllis had now taken to wearing on the course.

Mr Captain now regarded Phyllis, dressed in her purple mini skirt and pink Lycra top, a matching pink, purple and lilac polka-dotted bandana round her tumbling blonde locks, her long muscular legs freshly waxed, her tattooed arms, her whole body reeking of cheap perfume, and visibly shuddered. He was only grateful that her teeing off time was 11 a.m. and not 11.10. as the Mayor was due to arrive at 11.20. and 11.10. was a time far too close for comfort. If the Mayor were to see the monstrosity it would be the end! The end now proceeded to get a little nearer.

"Blooming heck I've forgotten my driver," Phyllis suddenly said to her partners. "The pro's been re-gripping it for me and I was supposed to pick it up."

"Well you haven't got time to go back, Phyllis" said Simpson, checking his watch. "We're due off in less than two minutes."

"Can't you drive with your two wood?" suggested Hawker, helpfully.

Phyllis shook her head. "No, a girl needs her driver."

Alfred Jacobson, who was in the following threesome and had arrived at the tee early, now spoke up. "Why not go back and get it Phyllis? I'll take your place and you can take mine."

Mr Captain was onto Jacobson's suggestion faster than a politician at the opening of a new pig trough. "Over my dead body he will!" he barked, tendentiously. "He stays in the threesome he is already in!" (When Phyllis had first become a woman she had requested everyone at the club to not only call her by her new name but to think of her as a woman as well. Mr Captain hadn't even tried to do either, and had steadfastly continued to call her Philip and refer to her as 'he'. Indeed he delighted in doing so.)

"What's wrong with me swapping with him?" demanded Phyllis.

Mr Captain didn't beat about the bush. In his opinion all transvestites and transsexuals should be put down, preferably painfully, along with all homosexuals of both sexes, and their remains thrown in a lime pit, and he didn't mind who knew it. "Because the Lord Mayor will be arriving soon," he said imperiously. "And I don't want him setting eyes on you. And I'm quite sure the Mayor himself wouldn't want to set eyes on you either if he knew the state of you."

"Oh I don't know about that, Mr Captain," said Simpson. "From what I've heard of the Mayor he likes a bit of skirt."

"Phyllis isn't a bit of skirt," grinned Hawker. "She's a lot of skirt. A great big joyous bundle of skirt."

"Why thank you, Martin," said Phyllis, fluttering her false eyelashes, "I didn't know you cared."

Mr Captain cringed at Phyllis's overt display of feminism, which only made him stick even more firmly to his guns. "So for the sake of the Mayor I insist you stick to your official starting time," he commanded.

"The Mayor," said Phyllis, with a flamboyant toss of her curls, "can kiss my bottom."

Hawker gave a lewd smile. "You can put me down for that too Phyllis."

"Get in the queue," said Simpson, joining in the fun.

"Down boys," said Phyllis. She turned to Jacobson. "Thanks for swapping with me Alf," she said, and set off for the pro's shop without further ado, leaving Mr Captain utterly distraught.

—៣—

"Hello hello hello, what's all this then?" said Harris, on the walk from the tee to the thirteenth green.

"What's all what?" said Garland.

Harris pointed at the adjoining twelfth fairway. "Plod."

Garland and Ifield looked across to see Constable Fearon, Constable James and Jason some hundred yards away making their way down the fairway in the opposite direction. Ifield recognised Jason immediately. "It's that kid you took prisoner, Mr Vice!"

"You're right," said Harris. "He said his dad was a policeman. The little bugger must have been telling the truth."

"Christ I can do without this," said Garland, annoyed. "I've got a good round going."

"I don't think they'll bother too much about that if I know coppers," said Ifield. "They can be mean bastards when they want to be."

"They're walking away from us anyway," observed Harris. "Perhaps they'll miss us."

"Let's just hope so," said Garland.

—៣—

On the eleventh green Armitage settled over his putt, if the verb settled can be ascribed to someone whose current state of mind was about as stable as a ping pong ball going over Niagara Falls. Thankfully the double vision that had plagued him for the last couple of holes had completely disappeared. When it had been restored to normal Armitage had breathed a huge sigh of relief. Taking an apprehensive sharp intake of breath would have been more appropriate, for the brief spell of normal vision had quickly been replaced by what can only be described as phallus vision. And accompanying the phallus vision came the suspicion that what Grover had said to him earlier, that he had dicks on the brain, might somehow be true. In fact he knew it to be true, he had seen evidence of it with his own eyes.

He now saw evidence of it again as the head of his Ping putter struck the ball, and, as the ball set off for the hole some twelve feet away, proceeded to elongate itself into a six inch long, golf ball-wide, penis. As Armitage watched its journey to the hole, mouth agape, eyes stuck out like chapel hat pegs, the penis sprouted a couple of golf ball-sized testicles. Then, as the hole got nearer the penis got bigger, until at the moment it entered the hole it was the same diameter, and a perfect fit, the shaft of the penis disappearing up to the hilt, leaving the testicles above ground.

"Oh well holed," said Stock, as the penis disappeared. He approached the hole, flagstick in hand. "Stay there, I'll throw it back to you."

With that Stock retrieved the penis and tossed it back to Armitage. By now it was fully eighteen inches long. Armitage instinctively dropped his putter and held out his hands wide enough to enable him to catch something of this size. However by the time it arrived it was a normal-sized golf ball again. Passing through his outstretched hands it hit him on the chest and dropped harmlessly to the ground.

—ᴡ—

"Han Ging Li."
"Lou Sinpediment."
"Caz Hywel Water."

—ᴡ—

When Fidler had started to make his way from the course after running out of balls he had every intention, as he had intimated to Dawson and Elwes, of going to the pro's shop to buy some more. However on the way there it struck him what a pointless exercise this would be. After all he had only five more holes to play and even if he happened by some miracle to get a hole in one at each of them his play had been so poor on the previous thirteen holes he would still have no chance of winning. Apart from that he had things to do, the lawn needed mowing for one and his VAT return needed to be filled in for another. Of course Dawson and Elwes would be waiting for him to return, and if he were to go home they would be waiting until the cows came home, which was something to be considered. However, on reflection, far from this being an obstacle to his going home he saw it as all the more reason for him to do so in view of the spiteful trick they'd played on him. So he went home.

—⚬—

In the beer tent Mr Harkness, Mr Oldknow and Mr Wormald were already well into their third double whisky with pint of bitter chaser and things were livening up. The Lady Captain, who was matching them with double gins but eschewing the pints of bitter in favour of more double gins, had just succeeded in bringing the gentlemen's conversation on the subject of crown green bowls round to the subject of sex, a quantum leap by any stretch of the imagination, but nothing to a woman who has taken a shine to someone.

"Taller men make the best lovers," she said, looking fondly at Harkness, then added, modestly, "Or so I have been told."

"Really?" said Harkness, genuinely surprised.

"So I'm led to believe." The Lady Captain looked him up and down appreciatively. "You're quite a tall man, aren't you Mr Harkness."

"Quite tall, yes."

"I'm not, but I'm prepared to stand on a box," said Oldknow.

"Me too," said Wormald.

"Of course that isn't to say that shorter men can't be excellent lovers too," said the Lady Captain to Oldknow and Wormald, aware that Harkness might not feel the same way about her as she felt about him, and hedging her bets.

At almost sixty years of age the Lady Captain was still a very attractive woman so Oldknow and Wormald wasted no time in encouraging her further.

"It's not the size of the gun...." said Oldknow.

"....It's the force of the bullet," said Wormald.

"Quite," said the Lady Captain. She re-crossed her legs, making sure the three old men seated opposite her got a good view of a generous expanse of creamy white thigh and hopefully a glimpse of her pink silk French knickers. "Of course my husband Bobby was a tall man. He was an excellent lover."

"I wouldn't expect a man who said a pint of bitter always went down better when it was accompanied by a chaser to be anything else," said Oldknow, sagely.

"Me neither," said Wormald.

"But of course he's sadly passed on, and...." the Lady Captain said, sadly, leaving the rest of the sentence unspoken.

Oldknow filled it in as "I'm going short."

Wormald, a coarser man, filled it in as "I'm gasping for the leg over."

Harkness, a less worldly man and more of a gentleman than his companions, didn't fill it in at all. His late wife had kept him just as short of sex as she had of alcohol and it had been so long since he'd had it he had almost forgotten it existed. Certainly any play for his affections would have to be couched in more obvious terms than "But of course he's sadly passed on, and...."

The Lady Captain now sensed that her words, while bringing more than a twinkle to the eye of Oldknow, and nothing short of a lascivious grin and the beginnings of an erection from Wormald, had had no effect at all on Harkness. She decided to adopt a less oblique approach. She got up, walked over to him, sat on his knee, put her arms round his neck, and said, "How about a fuck?"

—⁂—

Mr Captain had just about recovered from the upset of Phyllis Hill when the fire engine drove onto the course.

It wasn't the first time Mr Captain had seen a fire engine on the golf course; a few years previously during a period of drought the local fire service had been good enough to pump thousands of gallons of water over the greens and fairways in an effort to stop them burning up. However there was no drought at the moment, and even if there had been and the course had been drier than the Sahara Desert nobody would have sent for the fire service to pump water over it today, not on Captain's Day.

In fact Tobin, who observed the appearance of the fire engine through the pro's shop window, would himself have sent for the fire service to pump water over the course if he'd thought of it. However he wasn't too disappointed at not thinking of it as he'd thought of something much, much better.

Mr Captain quickly headed for the fire engine, waving his arms about in an effort to make it stop. It would have stopped anyway, as the driver of the fire engine, Leading Fireman Jeffers, needed directions. After pulling up and waiting for Mr Captain to walk round to his side of the cab the fire officer wound down the window and said, "Excuse me, which is the way to the thirteenth green?"

Not for the first time that day, nor the last, Mr Captain couldn't believe his ears. "What?"

"The thirteenth green. Apparently you have a woman stuck up a tree."

"A woman?"

"The Lady Captain-Erect, I believe. Nine nine nine call. Usually it's cats stuck up trees, a woman will make a nice change, give me the chance to practice my fireman's lift. That's difficult on cats."

Mr Captain was apoplectic. "You can't go onto the golf course with a fire engine just to get a woman down from a tree!"

Blakey, the other fireman in the cab, leaned over. "Just how long do you think our ladder is, mate?"

"What?"

"Well we can't reach her from here, can we? So stop messing about and tell us where the thirteenth green is, we've got a job to do."

In view of the imminent arrival of the Mayor Mr Captain considered refusing point blank to tell the firemen the whereabouts of the thirteenth green in the hope they would turn round and go away, then dismissed the idea, realising that if he didn't tell them someone else was sure to. He glanced at his watch. Almost ten past eleven. The thirteenth green was quite some distance away. By the time the fire engine had made its way there and rescued the Lady Captain-Elect the Mayor could very well have made his visit and departed for his next appointment. In addition he was mindful that the emergency services didn't seem to have much sense of direction when it came to golf courses, if the policemen who had recently arrived back at the first tee twenty minutes after leaving it were anything to go by, and that there was an excellent chance the fire engine would be out on the golf course and out of sight for quite some time, so all things considered he decided to be helpful. "It's over there," he said, pointing in the approximate direction of the thirteenth green. "No hurry."

—⁊⁊⁊—

On regaining consciousness Millicent wondered what on earth she was doing lying stretched out on the ground behind the beer tent with a couple of cans of lager, thoughtfully placed there by Oldknow, supporting her head as a sort of alcoholic pillow. She searched her mind for some clue. The last thing she could remember was being in the beer tent when she had introduced her father and his two friends to the Lady Captain and had asked them what they would like to drink. She suddenly sat bolt upright as she recalled what had happened next. That revolting song had been played! And at such a deafening volume that the whole golf course must have heard it! She glanced at her watch. Good Lord, it must have been over twenty minutes ago. She leapt to her feet. Daddy Rhythm would have to be dealt with forthwith! He would have to go! She would bring her record player and allow that to provide the music for the dance that evening, or employ her next-door neighbour's seven-year-old to provide it on his toy trumpet, anything rather than risk that detestable Daddy Rhythm reprobate playing his horrible music again.

She rolled up her sleeves and set off for the clubhouse, so intent on dealing with the Daddy Rhythm situation that she failed to notice the sounds of merriment emanating from within the beer tent. If she had heard Wormald's cry of "Get 'em off!" she might have made dealing with the awful Daddy Rhythm her second priority. But unfortunately she didn't.

"Well you can't join us and that's all there is to it," said Jerold Fredericks.

Phyllis appealed to Summers for support. "How do you feel about it, Sid?"

Most of the male members at Sunnymere treated the Phyllis Hill situation as a bit of a giggle and had no objection to playing with her. Fredrickson however was not one of them. "It doesn't matter a monkey's doo-dah how Sid feels about it," he said, before Summers could reply, "I'm not playing golf with a man who's had his tackle cut off and dresses up like a woman, and that's all about it."

Very often people who have been made aware they aren't wanted, as Phyllis had just so comprehensively been by Fredericks, choose not pursue the matter further and quietly let the matter drop. However Phyllis loved her golf almost as much as she loved being a woman, so stuck manfully, or perhaps womanfully, to her guns, and stood up to Fredericks. "I have a perfect right," she said, pushing out her artificial chest.

"No you haven't," said Fredericks.

"Or a perfect left," added Summers, with a grin.

"What?" said Fredericks.

"Her breasts. They're neither of them perfect, they're falsies."

Fredericks eyed his playing partner reproachfully. "This is nothing to joke about, Sid."

"I was only saying," said Summers, a little shamefaced.

Fredericks admonished him. "Well don't." He turned his attention to Phyllis. "So kindly clear off and let us get on with our game."

Phyllis wasn't about to give up so easily. She had noticed Mr Captain hovering nearby and now, employing the feminine wiles she seemed to have gained when she acquired her vagina and blonde wig she said, "I think we should let Mr Captain decide whether or not I can play with you," then added, artfully, "It is his Captain's Day, after all." With that she turned to Mr Captain, gave him the benefit of a sweet smile, and said, "*Do* you think I should be allowed play with Sid and Jerold, Mr Captain?"

At that moment there was only one thing in the whole world that Mr Captain would have liked more than for Phyllis to join Sid and Jerold and for the three of them to get themselves up the fairway and out of view of the Mayor as rapidly as possible, and that was for Phyllis to be struck by a bolt of lightning and reduced to a pile of smouldering cinders, but as that happy happening didn't seem likely he had no alternative but to side with Phyllis. "Yes Philip, I do think you should be allowed to play with Jerold and Sid," he said, then added, with a meaningful look at Fredericks, "In fact I insist upon it. And that is my final decision."

"There you are," said Phyllis, with the little pout she had been practising, "Mr Captain says you have to let me play with you."

Fredericks however was made of just as stern a stuff as Phyllis. "Mr Captain," he said firmly, "can take a hike. And you Phyllis can go with him."

Phyllis was nothing if not stubborn, especially when it came to defending her rights as a woman and a golfer. She regarded Fredericks coolly for a moment, then said, "I intend, as you will soon discover Jerold, to do precisely the opposite of taking a hike. Because if I'm not going to be allowed to play then nobody else will be allowed to play," and with that she lay down on the ground between the tee markers, all six feet two inches of her, effectively stopping anyone from driving off the tee.

—⟋⟍—

"Juan Under."
"Al Bertrosstoo
"Sick Zover."

—⟋⟍—

Playing the seventeenth Arbuthnott, still having the game of his life, was three over par gross, and heading for a finishing score of something like a net fifty six, a remarkable achievement by any standards. Even if he were to have a disaster of Jean Van der Velde proportions at the eighteenth he would still come in with something like a net sixty, an excellent score round the reasonably difficult Sunnymere course with its four large ponds, all of which came into play at numerous holes, and better by three strokes than the score Alec Adams intended to put in.

Naturally Arbuthnott was as pleased as punch with his round and even though he had promised himself that he wouldn't boast about his performance any more for fear of Chapman accusing him of crowing again he couldn't resist just a small crow as his approach shot hit the green in the regulation two strokes and came to rest in the two putt zone. "Well," he said, slotting his six iron back into his bag, "a four at the last and I reckon the trophy will be mine. If it isn't already."

Chapman, whose chances of winning had disappeared about seven holes back along with whatever good grace he had left, was onto Arbuthnott like a shot. "I thought you were going to give over crowing? But no, there you go again. You just can't help yourself can you."

"What do you mean, again?" Arbuthnott protested. "I haven't crowed once since the eighth green. I deliberately haven't crowed."

"You don't have to, you've been strutting about like a cockerel for the last half hour."

"Anyway I wasn't crowing. I was just making the point that if I two putt this green and get a four at the last the trophy will be mine."

"*If* you two putt this green and get a four at the last."

Unfortunately, having permitted himself a little crow, Arbuthnott had developed the taste for it again. "There's no way I'll three putt this green the way I'm putting, Gerry," he crowed. "And even if I took a five or a six at the last, which I won't, I would still win the Captain's Day trophy by a mile."

"Crow, crow crow," said Chapman. "Crow crow, bloody crow."

Arbuthnott gave a shrug of his shoulders. "Be like that if it makes you feel any better. But I'm just stating a fact. Nothing can stop me now." Never would the expression 'famous last words' prove to be more appropriate.

—∞—

The regular job of helicopter pilot Brian Green was to take groups of up to four people on pleasure flights round the Derbyshire Dales. It was work that paid handsomely but after well over a thousand such flights was a job that bored him to death. Boring it might have been but he was finding that flying his helicopter round and round the restricted range of the eighteen holes of Sunnymere golf course to be infinitely worse.

Whilst searching his mind for something to relieve the monotony of his task he had recalled that it had been quite amusing when his helicopter had suddenly appeared as if from nowhere and frightened the golfers putting out on the third green. Unable to come up with anything that offered a better prospect of light relief he decided to try a similar manoeuvre again. When he did, as Thompson, Livermore and Purseglove were putting out, the reaction of the golfers was even more amusing than it had been the first time he'd done it. Thompson had shrieked and dropped to his knees, shielding himself as if from some monster in a horror movie, Livermore had stood stock still, absolutely mortified, and peed in his trousers, whilst Purseglove, in an effort to get out of the way, had tripped over his own feet, fallen headlong into a bunker and ended up with a mouthful of sand. In the cockpit Green had roared with laughter. Martin Morton, the man videoing the proceedings, had also found the incident quite amusing and had joined in the laughter. However, being a golfer himself, he at least had the decency to stop filming.

—∞—

Having herself fainted not too long ago Millicent thought the same fate had befallen Phyllis on approaching the first tee and seeing her lying there, but on her arrival she could clearly see otherwise. A distressed Mr Captain quickly filled her in with the details as to why, then went on, "This could spoil my day, Millicent. No one will be able to tee off while that thing insists on lying there."

"Well you have my every sympathy darling, which goes without saying, but I really don't see what I can do about it," said Millicent. "Apart from that I have problems of my own. I have that wretched Daddy Rhythm person to sort out."

"If it is to chastise him I was about to do that myself half-an-hour ago but found that the yobbo had already left. So if you could perhaps have a word with Philip, Millicent, now you have the time? Promise him you'll allow him to play in the ladies' competition in future perhaps? No need to fulfil that undertaking of course. Anything to move him off...." Mr Captain suddenly cut off what he was about to say in favour of a strangulated cry of "Good Lord!" and his demeanour changed in an instant from very worried to the verge of panic.

"What on earth's the matter Henry?" said Millicent, alarmed.

"The press! The press are here already." Mr Captain pointed over Millicent's shoulder.

Millicent turned to see Derbyshire Dales Times reporter Ed Eagles accompanied by staff photographer Ben Booth heading towards them.

"Quick, we'll have to head them off," said Mr Captain, "We can't have them seeing Philip, you know what the press is like."

Millicent knew only too well what the press was like. Fortunately she also knew what was almost guaranteed to divert them. "I'll take them to the beer tent for a free drink," she said, "Keep them well out of the way until the Mayor arrives."

With that Mr Captain and Millicent quickly closed in on the two press men. "Good morning, gentlemen," called Mr Captain, sounding a lot more cheerful than he felt. "You've arrived in good time I see."

"Why is that woman lying down on the first tee?" asked Eagles, peering over Mr Captain's shoulder, before Millicent could sidetrack him with an offer of liquid refreshment.

"What woman?" said Mr Captain, looking hopefully in exactly the opposite direction to the first tee, just in case there was a woman over there doing something slightly less embarrassing, who he could palm off on Eagles.

"There's a big blonde bird lying on the first tee."

"How about a drink, gentlemen?" said Millicent, taking hold of Eagles' arm and attempting to steer him towards the beer tent.

The reporter pushed Millicent's hand away. "Hold on, hold on a minute. What's the story with the blonde chick?"

"Nothing," said Mr Captain. "No story at all. He just fainted."

"He?"

"My husband means 'she'," said Millicent, quickly. "Now if you'd like to...."

But Eagles had already pushed his way past Millicent and was heading purposefully for the first tee, followed by Booth, his camera at the ready, hopeful of getting a good crotch shot. Mr Captain watched them go, helpless to stop them. He let out a deep, forlorn sigh, for he knew what the outcome would be; an unsavoury article in the next edition of the Derbyshire Dales Times once Eagles had discovered that Phyllis used to be a man, which journalists being journalists he was bound to. The only good thing about it was that whatever the reporter wrote it wouldn't appear until the next edition of the newspaper the following Friday, and therefore it couldn't spoil his day.

The thought cheered him up a little and he began to feel a little better about things. After all, he told himself, although there had been one or two unsavoury incidents which he could have done without, none of them had really spoiled his day. And nothing *would* spoil his day, he now vowed, taking a firmer hold on himself, whatever the Gods might throw at him. With that he threw back his shoulders and tilted his chin, in the manner he had once seen Neil Hamilton do when facing adversity, and made ready to face the rest of his day.

—⁂—

Armitage took his stance and addressed the ball, which at the moment was still a ball. Which is more than can be said for the seven iron in his hands, which, since he'd taken it from his bag to play his approach shot, had metamorphosed into a four feet long penis. He closed his eyes tightly and tried with every nerve in his body and every cell in his addled brain to will the penis into becoming a seven iron once again but when he re-opened them he saw that it had steadfastly remained a penis. In an effort to try to fool it into thinking it was a golf club again he waggled it. A mistake, as immediately he started waggling it so it began to stiffen and grow, and as it stiffened and grew the end of it rose upwards and in a matter of seconds was pointing almost skywards. Letting out a strangled scream he threw it high in the air.

"What on earth is the matter Trevor?" enquired the six feet penis in the baseball cap stood watching him.

"There's definitely something the matter with him, George," said the slightly shorter but thicker bareheaded penis.

"George?" Armitage said to himself. "What does it mean, George? Penises aren't called George, they're called Dick or Percy or Willy or John Thomas, I've never heard of one called George before."

"He doesn't look too good to me," said the six feet penis. "Maybe it would be as well if we sat him down for a bit and got someone to take a look at him."

"Doctor Jackman is in the threesome behind us, let's ask him if he'll give him the once over," said the slightly shorter but thicker penis.

The two penises began to approach Armitage, who immediately cowered and started backing away from them, his arms raised in front of him to fend them off. "Get away from me you pricks!" he shouted, then turned and hared off back down the fairway as fast as his legs would carry him.

Mr Captain and Millicent were waiting outside the clubhouse when the Mayoral limousine drew up, right on time. They both stepped forward, all beams, as the chauffeur opened the door and the Lord Mayor and Lady Mayoress alighted.

"Welcome to Sunnymere Golf Club," said Mr Captain, offering his hand.

The Mayor shook Mr Captain's hand but seemed far more interested in what was happening on the first tee. He pointed at it. "What's going on over there?" Fortunately the five minutes that had elapsed since Ed Eagles had gone to interview Phyllis had given Mr Captain the chance to think up a reasonably believable explanation for the scene on the first tee. "The lady prostrate on the tee is the official starter," he replied. "Unfortunately she was hit by a stray golf ball."

The Mayor raised an eyebrow. "Really? How unfortunate. I must go to her and offer her my commiserations."

"No!" said Mr Captain, panic-stricken. "No, there isn't time. I've just noticed a threesome come off the ninth green and make their way towards the beer tent, and they happen to be three men I'd particularly like you to meet."

"It won't take a minute," said the Lord Mayor, anxious not to miss an opportunity of getting a close-up of a big titted-blonde lying on the ground, probably showing her knickers.

"Maybe later, Herbert," said the Lady Mayoress. She knew her husband all too well and was well aware that he would be offering the big-titted blonde quite a

1 7 1

bit more than his commiserations if he got half the chance.

"Of course dear," said the Lord Mayor, reluctantly.

—⁂—

"Hey up, trouble," said Harris, looking back down the fairway from the fourteenth green.

By the expedient of walking each hole in turn from the first tee the two policemen and Jason had finally arrived on the same hole as Garland, Harris and Ifield, despite having had to stop for ten minutes whilst James had a rest. As yet they were too far away from their quarry to recognise them as such but that moment wouldn't be too long in coming, provided of course that James didn't feel the need of another rest.

"Shit!" said Garland, on seeing the policemen. "I stand a chance of winning this as well."

"Well I don't much fancy your chances of winning it now, Mr Vice," said Ifield. "I mean a child abuse charge?"

"Child abuse? What are you talking about? I only tied him to my trolley for God's sake."

"I don't think his dad will see it that way," said Harris. "The fuzz are very keen on child abuse nowadays."

Ifield piled on the agony. "Especially if it's their own kid that's the victim of the abuse."

"Automatic custodial offence I should think," said Harris.

Garland swallowed. "Prison?"

"I wouldn't bet against it," said Ifield. "And we all know what happens to child abusers when they get banged up, don't we?" He thought that Garland would have a fair idea, but Ifield, one of those individuals who seem to take a delight in his fellow man's discomfort, told him anyway. "Put it this way, I'd rather have my arsehole than yours after you've been inside for a week or two."

"Shit a brick!"

"You might well be able to when you've been inside for a week or two and your arsehole has been stretched."

Garland reacted angrily. "Will you just shut it, things are bad enough as it is!"

172

Garland, as anxious to hold on to his anal virginity as the next man, or most next men, now looked wildly around for somewhere to hide. Trees were abundant at Sunnymere, many of them large oaks, easily wide enough for a man to hide behind with comfort, and Garland would have hidden behind one, or better still up one and safely concealed in its uppermost branches, but unfortunately the fourteenth was one of the few holes that didn't have any trees. It did however have a pond, and very close by too, about twenty yards from the green at its nearest point. What's more, Garland now noted, the pond had several large clumps of reeds at its edge in which a man might hide himself. He glanced quickly back down the fairway. The policemen were about a couple of hundred yards away so he certainly couldn't afford to hang about.

"Tell them I've gone," he said, quickly beginning to slip out of his clothes.

"What are you going to do?" said Harris.

"You'll see. If they ask you where I am tell them I had to leave the course, sick. Which isn't too far from the bloody truth."

Now down to his underpants he stuffed his clothes into the pocket of his golf bag, tossed the bag into the bunker at the back of the green, then hurried to the pond and stepped into it, near to one of the clumps of reeds. The water came up to mid thigh. Despite the warm weather the water was quite cold and it took his breath for a moment. He quickly snapped off a two feet section of reed then, needing all the breath he could muster for what he had in mind, he inhaled deeply, put one end of the reed in his mouth, then lay down in the water amongst the clump of reeds.

"He'll drown himself," said Harris, alarmed.

"No," said Ifield. "He put a reed in his mouth."

"What?"

"To breathe through."

"Will he be all right then?"

"Oh yes. It's very effective. I once saw Tarzan do it in a film. Tarzan and the Leopard Women I think. And Sabu, he did it too; can't remember the film though."

—⚌—

173

"Frank Fart."

"Frank Wetfart."

"Frank Shitimself."

—⁂—

Arbuthnott had been driving well all morning but his drive at the eighteenth was his best yet, two hundred and forty yards straight down the middle, almost to the corner of the slight dogleg, in perfect position for his approach shot to the green. He turned to Chapman, flapped his arms as though they were wings, scratched the floor with one of his feet, and crowed, "Cock-a-doodle-doo."

"Bollocks," said Chapman.

—⁂—

"Jessica?" called Fidler, at the foot of the stairs.

Fidler had expected his wife to be in when he arrived home from the golf course, she usually was. He checked the kitchen but she wasn't there either, then opened the back door to see if she was in the garden. He called out again but there was no response. "Must have slipped out somewhere," he said to himself, when his call prompted no reply. He hoped she wouldn't be long in coming back because he'd decided to use the spare time he now had on his hands to go with her to pick the new hall carpet they planned on buying and save themselves the trouble of having to do it in the afternoon, as they'd planned.

Upstairs Southfield paused in his labours astride Fidler's wife and cocked an ear at the door.

"What's the matter?" said Jessica. "Why have you stopped?"

"I'm sure I heard somebody call your name," whispered Southfield, worry lines creasing his brow.

"It was you, you get carried away, 'Jessica, Jessica, I'm going to take you to the moon,' you said. Well keep going Captain Kirk, we're not there yet."

Southfield listened for a moment more. "Must have imagined it," he said, then carried on with his lunar mission.

174

It was the third time they'd had sex that morning. They were naked again this time. Well he was, she was almost naked; at his request she'd left on her boots from the second time they'd had sex, when she'd dressed up as Lara Croft, Tomb Raider.

In fact it was the boots which were the first thing that Fidler saw when he stepped into the bedroom. He'd bought them for Jessica only a couple of weeks previously for her birthday. At first he thought he was seeing things, as the boots appeared to be hanging upside down in mid-air, before it registered in his brain that Jessica's legs were in them. And a moment later that someone was in Jessica.

The man, whoever he was, had his back to him. Jessica, eyes closed, was moaning something about landing on the Moon and how she was nearly there and looking forward to his Moonshot. They never touched down. What stopped her, and her lover, was the single shouted word 'So!' Fidler felt really foolish when he shouted it, feeling it made him sound like the cuckold in a Victorian melodrama, but he couldn't think of anything more appropriate to say.

It didn't really matter, whatever he had said would have stopped Southfield and Jessica, probably even 'Carry on fucking'. Jessica opened her eyes, saw Fidler and screamed. The man turned his head to him. Fidler recognised him immediately and, sounding once again like a wronged husband in a Victorian melodrama cried out, "Southfield!"

There was nothing Victorian or melodramatic in the way Southfield now disengaged himself from Jessica faster than shit off a shovel and leapt off the bed, it was one hundred per cent twenty first century kitchen sink realism. As was his pathetic excuse. "It isn't what you think," he blurted out, pulling at the sheet in an effort to cover his nakedness.

"Oh? Well I was thinking you were shagging my wife, so if you weren't shagging my wife perhaps you can put me right and enlighten me as to what exactly you *were* doing?" said Fidler, now having regained his full power of speech and putting it to good effect.

"I...I mean..."

Southfield never got the chance to say what he meant because Fidler now lunged forward and made a grab for him. Southfield just managed to avoid him, causing him to slip and fall to the floor, and whilst his adversary was disoriented seized the opportunity to make a run for it. Fidler cursed, picked himself up and gave chase.

—〜〜—

"Are you all right now, love?" said Leading Fireman Jeffers, when he and Fireman Blakey had eventually managed to get Mrs Quayle down from the tree.

"Nothing that a good kick in Mr Irwin's testicles won't put right," said Mrs Quayle, brushing twigs, leaves and the remnants of a thrush's nest off her clothes.

Jeffers winced at the thought. "I think we'd better give you a lift back to the clubhouse, get them to phone for a doctor, just to be on the safe side."

"Oh can I come too?" said Mrs Salinas. "I've always wanted to ride in a fire engine."

"Me too," said Mrs Rattray. "Please? And please may I ring the bell?"

"Didn't you say something about doing the measuring in the Nearest the Pin competition?" said Blakey.

"Oh never mind that," said Mrs Salinas. "They can do their own measuring after what that *man* did to poor Mrs Quayle. Apart from that the whole business has given me quite a shock, so I may have to be looked at too."

"I'm feeling a little fragile myself," added Mrs Rattray. "All this fuss and bother, I need my blood pressure checked at the very least."

"Well it'll be a bit cramped, but I suppose we can manage," said Jeffers. "Hop in."

—〜〜—

The lorry with the load of twenty tons of manure that Tobin had ordered over the phone a short while ago now

176

drove onto the course. Tobin, watching through the pro's shop window with Darren, smiled to himself.

Without pause the lorry drove onto the middle of the eighteenth green and deposited its load, then drove off, leaving behind a steaming pile of horse muck approximately ten feet high by twenty feet wide, between the greenside bunker and the flagstick.

"Awesome," said Darren.

—⚶—

By the time Harris and Irwin had putted out the two policemen and Jason had reached the green.

Jason pointed an accusing finger at them. "Them two blokes were playing with him."

Fearon eyeballed Harris. "So where's your mate then?"

"Mate?"

"The bloke you were playing your stupid bloody game with?"

"Oh, Mr Vice you mean."

"Yes, Mr bloody Vice. Where is the bastard?"

"He was having a bad round so he ripped up. Said he had better things to do."

"That I can believe. Anything is a better thing to do than golf. Any idea where he might be?"

"You could try the nineteenth hole."

Fearon's eyes glinted. "Have I to get my truncheon out?"

"What?"

"I might not know too much about your pansy game but I do know there's only eighteen holes in it."

"The nineteenth hole is the name we give to the bar," Harris explained, loftily.

Fearon grunted. "Typical. And he could be there, right?"

"Well he usually calls in for a couple before he goes."

Fearon turned to Jason. "These two wankers didn't abuse you as well, did they?"

"No we bloody well didn't!" protested Ifield. "Anyway he was pinching balls."

"I'll pinch your balls if you don't shut it, shit for brains" said Fearon, then turned to James. "Let's go."

James was looking around. "Is there a toilet round here?"

Ifield rolled his eyes. "We're in the middle of a golf course."

"There isn't a toilet?"

"Well of course there isn't."

"What do you do when you want a piss then?"

"Golfers do piss, do they?" said Fearon, with a sneer. "When they're not walking about looking like Rupert Bear?"

Harris ignored the slight. "You have to go behind a tree or a wall."

James looked around for a tree or a wall but there weren't any nearby. There was a pond though. Fearon noticed it. "Piss in there," he said. "Kill some pond life."

Constable James went over to the pond's edge and without ceremony started to urinate in it.

James was a man who preferred to direct his spray of urine around playfully rather than let it all land in the same spot, and on this occasion he was able to enjoy this extra-curricular pursuit more than usual as normally there were just toilet disinfectant blocks and cigarette ends or whatever else people had thrown in the urinal, to aim at; the pond however offered much more variety as a target for his projectile of pee, and after giving a frog on a lily pad a thorough dowsing he narrowly missed bringing down a dragonfly in mid-flight. Making a second attempt to ground the dragonfly only resulted in him peeing on his boots and the bottoms of his trousers, so he quickly abandoned the idea and chose as his next target a small fish at the edge of the clump of reeds that Garland happened to be lying in. Unfortunately for Garland the stickleback at which James now directed his waterfall was immediately over the vice-captain's head and it wasn't long before a generous amount of the constable's urine went down the reed that Garland had in his mouth. Garland's reaction was spontaneous and immediate. Spluttering and choking on James' warm pee, coughing his lungs up, he suddenly erupted from the pond looking for all the world like the Monster of the Lost Lagoon, except that when the monster emerged from the lost lagoon its underpants hadn't filled with water and weren't falling round its knees.

"Of course," said Ifield to Harris, "when Tarzan stuck a reed in his mouth and hid in the pond he didn't have a copper pissing on him."

Garland didn't hang about once his watery hiding place had been revealed. Visions of sharing a prison cell with a cellmate who was hung like a donkey and had a penchant for bottoms made him leap out of the pond even faster than Southfield had just leapt out of Jessica's bed, and pausing only to haul up his waterlogged y-fronts he hared off down the fairway faster than Usain Bolt with his behind on fire.

—∿—

From where his ball had come to rest Arbuthnott didn't have a view of the green, but it didn't really matter; he had played the eighteenth hole at Sunnymere hundreds of times so knew exactly the whereabouts of the green. A four iron over the corner of the dogleg would get him there today, he judged, taking the slight breeze against into account. He took out the chosen club, struck the ball as sweetly as he had ever struck a ball in his life, and the ball sped arrow-like for its target.

Just as Arbuthnott had known exactly where the green was he was now equally certain his ball would end up slap bang in the middle of it. What he didn't know, but was very soon to find out, was that also slap bang in the middle of the green was the huge pile of steaming manure.

—∿—

The memory of the vision that greeted Mr Captain and Millicent as they led the Lord Mayor into the beer tent - a living tableau of Mr Harkness, the Lady Captain on her knees fellating him, whilst at the same time masturbating Mr Oldknow and Mr Wormald who were standing either side of her, a sight which looked for all the world like some obscene animated coat of arms, a woman genuflecting with three men rampant - would haunt them to their dying day. In fact Millicent could have died there and then and if it had been left to her would have chosen to. Mr Captain's scream of horror came a split second before Millicent's scream of horror, but as if to make up for being the last to react Millicent's scream was louder and more piercing.

"What is it, what on earth's the matter?" said a concerned Lord Mayor, and then saw what was the matter. "Good Lord!" A moment or two later, managing to tear his eyes away from the sight set out before him, as he quite liked watching people perform sex acts and usually had to pay for the privilege, he turned to Mr Captain for an explanation. "What the devil is going on here, Fridlington?"

Much to Mr Captain's relief, for he was completely at a loss as to what to do or say, Millicent, a sharper knife than her husband, came to the rescue. "Gipsies," she said firmly, taking the Mayor and his lady by the arms and attempting to shepherd them away.

"Gipsies?

"Yes, they're a blasted nuisance. One only has to put up a tent and the next thing you know they've moved in. Exactly the same thing happened on Lady Captain's Day." She tugged on the Mayor's arm. "We'd best be off before they start trying to sell us some lucky white heather or pegs or something."

Resisting Millicent's efforts to move him on the Mayor turned to Mr Captain, puzzled. "But didn't you say you particularly wanted me to meet those people in the beer tent, Fridlington?"

Mr Captain had by now recovered enough to make some sort of answer. "Er....that's right," he said. "To demonstrate to you exactly what a huge problem these damned gipsies can be in the town. So that in your capacity of Lord Mayor you might be able to get the council to do something about it."

"So, now you have seen the extent of the problem Mr Mayor, can we please leave?" said Millicent, strengthening her grip on the Mayor's arm and re-doubling her efforts to lead him away from the terrible scene.

The Mayor was not about to depart that easily however. "I thought we were going to have a drink?" he said, not caring one way or the other if he had a drink, but wanting very much to see a bit more of the live sex show, which far from grinding to a halt on the Mayoral party's arrival had continued unabashed and had now increased in its intensity as all three old gentlemen neared their climax.

Millicent was a match for him. "There won't be any drink left; the gipsies will have drunk it all by now if I know anything about gipsies."

"And Millicent knows her gipsies," added Mr Captain. "So all in all I think the best thing we can do is repair to the eighteenth green without further delay." He glanced at his watch. "If I'm not mistaken the first threesome will be arriving anytime now, so we'll be just in time to greet them if we hurry."

—ᴍ—

Many of the holes at Sunnymere have tree-lined fairways, the trees serving not only to define the whole of the hole but also to provide it with a setting which is easy on the eye. Armitage would happily have settled for being on a fairway that had no trees at all, but whichever way he ran and no matter how many times he altered his course, he kept running into tree-lined fairways that were anything but easy on the eye, as through his eyes the fairways were lined not by trees but by tree-sized penises.

On the fairways themselves the dozen or so much smaller talking penises pulling golf trolleys which he had passed by and who had stopped, transfixed, to watch his progress, had said things to him like: "What's the matter, Trevor, what are you running away from?" and "Who's chasing you?" Armitage didn't stop to enlighten them, not even breaking stride in his eagerness to depart the phallus-infested hell in which he had found himself.

—⁓—

"Well bless my soul!" said Bagley, when he, Arbuthnott and Chapman had reached the eighteenth green, "It's a pile of horseshit!"

They had first seen the pile of manure when they had rounded the corner of the dogleg and the green came into view. At that distance, some hundred and fifty yards away, it was by no means clear what it was, although the smell, aided by the prevailing light breeze, might have given them a clue. Bagley had suggested it might be a new hazard, some sort of hillock, which had been secretly introduced overnight to make the closing hole more difficult, and that it might not be on the green at all, as it appeared to be, but either behind or in front of it. Once they had arrived at the green however and realised what the mound was composed of Chapman said that if it was indeed a hazard then it was a hazard he had no intention of ever venturing onto or into in order to join his ball if ever it should land in it. "What club could I use for my recovery shot?" he asked, not unreasonably, "A shit iron?"

Having checked the un-manured portion of the green, the greenside bunkers and behind the green, and discovering his ball to be in none of those locations, Arbuthnot said, "My ball must be in the manure because it's not on the green. What do you think I should do?"

"Send for a shit iron," said Chapman, enjoying himself now. "Tobin's bound to have one, he's got everything else."

"I don't think there's a rule that covers a heap of manure on the green," said Bagley, then added helpfully, "Unless of course you were to treat it as a loose impediment."

This suggestion pleased Chapman no end. "Well I'm not sure about it being an impediment but something must have been pretty loose to shit that lot," he chortled.

Bagley was more sympathetic to Arbuthnott's dilemma. "Perhaps you'd better declare it a lost ball and go back and play another one," he suggested.

"Like hell I will," said Arbuthnott, vehemently. "That would be a two stroke penalty. And even if I did there's no guarantee the same thing wouldn't happen again. Anyway it isn't lost, it's in that pile of manure."

"What are you going to do then?" said Bagley. "You're going to have to do something."

"Well we'll just have to find it, won't we. We've got five minutes."

"*We*?" said Chapman.

"Surely you're going to help me look for my ball?"

"You are joking, aren't you? It's in a pile of horseshit."

Arbuthnott could scarcely credit it, even of Chapman. "You don't mean to say you're going to leave it to me and Baggers to search for it on our own? When I'm within a gnat's whiskers of winning?"

"Er....." said Bagley, shaking his head.

Arbuthnott was aghast. "Not you too Baggers, surely?"

"Sorry Arby, you'll have to leave me out of this one, I'm allergic to manure."

"Since when?"

"Since he realised your ball was in a bloody great steaming heap of it," grinned Chapman.

Arbuthnott turned on Chapman. "It's nothing to gloat about, Gerry. This could cost me the competition."

"I thought you said you couldn't lose it?"

"Ah," said Arbuthnott. "I get it now. That's why you're refusing to help me, isn't it. Because I crowed a little about winning."

"I'm not helping you because I refuse point blank to scratch about in a pile of horseshit looking for your ball," said Chapman. "Your crowing didn't affect my decision in the slightest, it just made it easier to make."

"Well I don't refuse to scratch about in horseshit looking for my ball!" fumed Arbuthnott, and promptly stepped onto the pile of manure and started searching.

—⁓—

Fredericks had noticed the arrival of the manure, and as Phyllis wasn't showing any signs of vacating the first tee, and for want of something better to do, he had wandered over to the eighteenth green to take a closer look at it. Joining him in the inspection of the new feature were his playing partner Summers, the next threesome of John Huddlestone, Freddie Mickleover and Tony Sturgess, plus Derbyshire Dales Times staff Ed Eagles and Ben Booth (who had by now obtained an excellent crotch shot of Phyllis which he was going to email to the Daily Sport just as soon as he could get to his computer). Derbyshire Dales Radio reporter Dirk Kirk had in the meantime also arrived on the scene.

"Get a photograph of that," Eagles urgently instructed Booth, as soon as Arbuthnott had started scrambling around in the pile of manure like some demented dung beetle. "I don't know what's going on here but what with that sex change blonde picketing the first tee and this bloke playing around in a heap of horseshit I can sense a major story brewing here."

—⁓—

As Armitage raced along the phallus-lined purple fairway – purple at the moment that is, having previously been red, orange, black, ultramarine and all of these colours at the same time during the five minutes or so of his flight from the golf course – he never wanted to see or even think about another penis again as long as he lived. Death would be preferable to a life in which he had to see another dick. Or if the Grim Reaper wouldn't take pity on him and do him the favour of taking his life some other way of escape from the phalluses would do; if he couldn't outrun them perhaps some haven in which he could hide from them? Please? He was soon to have his wish, both wishes in fact, because as he ran down the eighteenth fairway towards the green, behind which ten more human being-sized penises were standing, such a haven presented itself. However it was to prove to be anything but a safe haven.

—⁓—

If nothing that had happened previously had failed to spoil Mr Captain's day completely then what he had just witnessed in the beer tent in the company of the Lord Mayor certainly had. The only consolation was that the Mayor didn't seem to have been too put out by it, so with a bit of luck his chances of becoming a councillor hadn't been damaged beyond repair. On his way to the eighteenth green he determined to demonstrate to the Mayor just what an important position the role of captain of a golf club was, and in particular how efficiently he was fulfilling that role. When he arrived there, only to see Arbuthnott standing wild-eyed atop a huge pile of manure feverishly scooping up large handfuls of it and sifting it through his fingers as if he was prospecting for gold, he wasn't at all sure if it represented an opportunity to display his skills of captaincy by dealing with the situation or an invitation to simply throw in the towel and take up brass rubbing.

Before he could make up his mind which of these options to take, the Mayor, displaying the powers of observation that had made him a power in local government, spoke up. "Isn't that a pile of manure?"

"Yes," said Mr Captain. He made no attempt to explain the appearance of the manure on the green in the forlorn hope that the Mayor was simply making an observation and not posing an embarrassing question.

The Mayor immediately dashed his hopes. "What's it doing there?"

"Fertilizer," said Millicent, coming to the rescue once again. "Summer dressing." She indicated Arbuthnott, who was still feverishly sifting handfuls of the manure. "That's the head greenkeeper." At that moment Armitage came hurtling into the picture from the side of the eighteenth fairway and dived head first into the pile of manure, disappearing up to his waist with a loud squelch. "And his assistant," Millicent continued. "As you can see, as eager to get stuck into his work as ever; that's the sort of dedicated staff we have here at Sunnymere."

—◊—

"There's that *man*!" shrieked Mrs Rattray, suddenly spotting Irwin.

Mrs Quayle looked in the direction in which Mrs Rattray was pointing and saw that her companion was correct; it was indeed the man who had put her in the tree.

The fire engine, driven by Jeffers, with Mrs Quayle, Mrs Rattray and Mrs Salinas seated alongside him in the cab and Blakey standing on the running board, was making its way down the edge of the sixteenth fairway. Fifty yards distant on the green Irwin was facing a difficult downhill putt to save his par. His life, as well as his putt, was soon to go downhill, and difficulties of a much greater magnitude were to engage his attention as Mrs Quayle, the glint of revenge in her eye, now suddenly grabbed hold of the steering wheel and wrenched it round so that the fire engine was pointing directly at Irwin.

"There *was* that man," she cried. "There *was* that man! Or soon will be!"

Realising Mrs Quayle's intentions, and having no wish to be cited as an accomplice on a charge of manslaughter, Jeffers took a firmer grip on the steering wheel and attempted to wrench it back. Mrs Quayle fought back spiritedly but Jeffers' superior strength told and he had just about managed to get the fire engine back on course when Mrs Salinas, as anxious as Mrs Quayle that Irwin should be punished for his sins, came to the assistance of her friend and commenced to beat Jeffers about the head with her handbag. When Jeffers let go of the wheel to protect himself Mrs Quayle was able to re-aim the fire engine squarely at Irwin once more, whilst Mrs Rattray, conscious of the fact that all Jeffers need do to prevent Mrs Quayle running down Irwin was to take his foot off the gas, dropped to the floor, grabbed hold of his foot and held it hard on the accelerator.

—⁂—

His worst fears realised, and trouser-less to boot, on fleeing from Jessica's bedroom Southfield had almost fallen down the staircase in his rush to put distance between himself and her husband. Having gained the back garden he had made his escape through the wicket gate which led directly onto the golf course, Fidler following him in hot and close pursuit.

Southfield was running in a blind panic, not heading anywhere in particular but simply trying to get away, so it was completely by accident that he now found himself on the eighteenth fairway heading towards the green.

—␣—

The same couldn't be said for Garland, who was also running down the eighteenth fairway towards the green with Constable Fearon in hot pursuit – Constable James having had to stop for a rest - as he knew exactly where he was heading. The eighteenth green was close to the exit to the course, which in turn was close to the car park, where his car was, and his car was both the sanctuary and the means of escape from the bastard of a policeman who was chasing him.

It hadn't yet occurred to him that he would be unable to get into his car, as he kept his keys in his trousers pocket and his trousers were in his golf bag which was back at the sixteenth green in a bunker, but then the minds of people who are being chased by a policeman are usually fully engaged in ensuring that the policeman doesn't catch up with them. However when the car park came into view, and his car with it, and he automatically reached for the keys in his trousers pocket, he realised that he hadn't got a trousers pocket, much less trousers, and was forced to make a hurried change in his plans.

—␣—

In fact Daddy Rhythm had not left the golf club, as Mr Captain had supposed. During the rendition of the final verse of I Don't Give a Toss the fuse in one of his amplifiers had blown, and rather than bring along a new fuse that evening he had elected to nip out and buy one and effect the repair there and then.

Now back, and with the new fuse in place, he decided to test it to ensure that the amplifier was working correctly. I Don't Give a Toss was still on the CD player but Daddy Rhythm, a man who took great pride in never repeating himself where his play list was concerned, decided to treat everyone to another of Lord Nose and the Bogies' hits, the seminal 'D'you Fancy a Shag?', a much louder, more dynamic number. The windows were still wide open and a minute later all one hundred and twenty decibels of Daddy Rhythm's rig were hitting all four corners of the golf course once again.

> D'you fancy a shag?
> Is that your bag?
> Or are you just leading me on?
> D'you fancy a shag?
> I won't call you a slag
> So how about me giving you one?
> So if you'd like some, cop this, babe

—⁓—

Listening to it, or more correctly trying not to listen to it, Mr Captain was absolutely mortified. Millicent was equally mortified, but on this occasion managed to hold on to consciousness. She would much rather have fainted again. Or preferably gone into a coma for a year or two. The Mayor, for the sake of the dignity of his office, tried to pretend he wasn't hearing it. His wife wasn't hearing it, as after hearing the first line she had stuck her fingers firmly in her ears. Several of the golfers greenside who were hearing it were smiling, whilst Fredericks was laughing out loud. Summers, a big fan of Lord Nose and the Bogies, joined in the singing.

Garland, with Fearon now within a couple of yards of catching him up, now ran on to the green, leapt onto the pile of manure and scrambled up its slippery slopes in an effort to reach its summit. He realised of course that Fearon would have him trapped, but was counting on his assailant not wishing to follow him up there, which would give him a little breathing space in which to figure a way out of the situation in which he had contrived to get himself.

Southfield, now reaching the eighteenth green and observing what Garland had done, came to much the same conclusion regarding his current situation vis-à-vis Fidler, and now joined Garland on the mountain of manure. Both Garland and Southfield had judged the situation correctly as Fidler, like Fearon, proved to be reluctant to follow, preferring to wait at base camp until something developed. They didn't have long to wait.

Mr Captain, sensing an enquiry from the Mayor as to why another two men had joined Arbuthnott and Armitage on the pile of manure, and taking a cue from his wife's inspiration of a moment or two ago, spread his arms expansively and said, "More greenkeepers. We really lavish attention on the greens here at Sunnymere."

"One of them is completely naked!" said the Mayor, astounded.

"Yes, just the one," said Mr Captain, as though the appearance of only one naked man on a pile of manure was the norm at Sunnymere and entirely acceptable.

"And the other one is wearing just his underpants."

"Yes, he's just an assistant."

"Thanks chaps, it's a Top Flight four," said Arbuthnott, to Garland and Fidler, too glad of a bit of help in the search for his ball to notice that the entire wardrobe of his helpers consisted of one pair of y-fronts.

Looking on, Fidler overheard Arbuthnott. Although he was prepared to bide his time getting his hands on Garland he wasn't about to put up with any more of this Top Flight four funny business. "Are you taking the piss?" he bellowed at Arbuthnott.

Arbuthnott turned to face him. "What?"

"You are, aren't you. You're taking the piss," said Fidler, and without bothering to wait for a reply scrambled up the pile of manure and punched Arbuthnott on the jaw, knocking him out cold.

—॰॰—

Right on cue, the helicopter had soared into view behind the third green as the threesome there were putting out. On this occasion however pilot Green had chosen the wrong men to upset. Tollemache, who had been putting at the time, and who the helicopter had caused to miss his putt, instead of cowering or falling over in surprise as the previous golfers had done, stood firm, drew back his arm, and threw his club at it. Fortunately it clattered into the fuselage and dropped harmlessly to the ground. However Burton's putter, which followed Tollemache's about a second later, whizzed past the cameraman's ear before hitting Green straight between the eyes, killing him instantly and leaving the helicopter spinning wildly out of control.

—॰॰—

D'you fancy a shag?
(If you're not on the rag)
Or are you just acting the fool?
D'you fancy a shag?
In the back of the Jag
Then I'll run you back to school
So if you'd like some, cop this, babe

—॰॰—

Having ripped up at the eleventh, having lost his ball and deeming it not worth his while going back to play another as his chances of winning had long since disappeared, Jones-Jones decided to give Cuddington's new swing a try, despite what had happened to Treforest when he had tried it. His reasoning was that he had nothing to lose now. Apart from that he had by now had the time to watch Cuddington's technique more closely and believed he could put it into practice. He'd already had a few practice swings with pleasing results. If anything it would be easier for him, he felt, as he made fewer swing mistakes going back than did Cuddington, so would consequently have fewer to make coming down, making his task that much easier.

He turned to Cuddington. "I'm thinking of g-giving your n-new swing a t-try."

"Well it's working for me a treat."

"R-right. I'll g-give it a g-go then."

Jones-Jones teed up and commenced to give it a go. However, as is generally the case, his actual swing was nowhere near the quality of his practice swings, and although he had more success than Treforest, inasmuch as he didn't hit his foot instead of the ball, he did hit the ball in such a manner that it set off from the tee in the direction of the eighteenth green in by far the wildest slice he had ever hit in his life.

—⁓—

Dogleg Davis, playing his approach to the ninth, didn't even have Jones-Jones's excuse that he was trying out something new to explain the violent hook he had just hit, which was now also homing in on the eighteenth green.

—⁓—

Irwin saw the fire engine bearing down on him when it was about thirty yards away. Horror-stricken he threw his putter in the air and raced off the green and down the fairway. By zig-zagging wildly as he ran he had so far been lucky enough to prevent the fire engine from flattening him. His luck now ran out when he suddenly found himself confronted by the pond beside the eighteenth green. Without even stopping to think about it he leapt into the shallow water, but too late, as the fire engine followed him in, running over him and killing him stone dead in an instant. Unable to stop, the fire engine ploughed on into the deeper water, where it sank with the loss of Mrs Rattray, Mrs Salinas and Fireman Blakey.

—⁓—

D'you fancy a shag?
No this isn't a gag
Or are you just taking the piss?
D'you fancy a shag?
You stupid little bag
If not you can suck on this
So if you'd like some, cop this, babe

—⁓—

Mr Captain surveyed the scene that during the last few moments had unfurled itself before him like all his worst nightmares rolled into one and then some. Although the Mayor hadn't said anything to him which would indicate otherwise he realised that his chances of becoming a councillor must surely have sunk along with the fire engine. Derbyshire Dales Radio's top presenter Dirk Kirk now stepped forward to inadvertently put the final nail in his coffin. He thrust his microphone under Mr Captain's nose. "With me here live at Sunnymere Golf Club, on wonderful Derbyshire Dales Radio, is the captain of the club, Henry Fridlington. Mr Captain, would you like to say a few words about events so far today?"

Mr Captain didn't have a single word that he'd like to say about events so far that day, let alone a few, but even if he'd had one it is doubtful whether he would have had the chance to say it before the helicopter suddenly plummeted from the skies and plunged upside down into the pile of manure. By flinging themselves clear at the last second Garland and Southfield just managed to save themselves from certain death, but nobody within a hundred yards managed to save themselves from being covered from head to foot in horseshit and shredded pieces of Armitage and Arbuthnott as the helicopter's propellers ploughed through the pile of manure, spraying it in all directions. Being right at the edge of the green, the Mayoral party received the brunt of it.

Before the Mayor had a chance to make a comment on this latest development Jones-Jones's ball hit him on the right-hand side of his forehead, a split second before

Dogleg Davis's ball hit him on the left side of his forehead. He dropped like a stone at Mr Captain's feet.

Mr Captain had a word to say now, although it wasn't one suitable to be broadcast. "Fuck!" he said, loud and clear into Dirk Kirk's microphone, for all those tuned in to Derbyshire Dales Radio to hear. "Fuck!" he repeated, for the Mayor, the Lady Mayoress, Bagley, Chapman, Garland, Fidler, Southfield, Fredericks, Huddlestone, Mickleover, Sturgess, Fearon, Eagles and Booth to hear. "Fuck fuck fuck fuck fuck fuck fuck FUCK!!"

And the following day he resigned.

Addendum

A further death occurred that day when the helicopter, after it had crashed on the eighteenth green, parted company with its rear propeller, which then flew through the air several hundred yards before coming down on the seventh green, whereupon it decapitated Alec Adams, instantly reducing the complement of Adams brothers to two and their nomenclature from triplets to twins – thus making it much harder in future for the surviving Adams brothers to cheat. Although wishing death on no one this was seen by the membership to be almost as good a thing as the demise of Mr Captain.

Following the carnage on the eighteenth green the Captain's Prize competition was abandoned. At the next monthly meeting of the General Committee it was decided that the competition would be shelved for the current year, but in an unprecedented gesture awarded the trophy posthumously to the late Andrew Arbuthnott in deference to the remarkable card he would probably have returned. His name is now up in gold.

John Hargreaves, Hon Sec

October 2009

FOOTBALL CRAZY

Superintendent Screwer fixed Sergeant Hawks with a beady eye. When would they ever learn? "Where there is football, Sergeant, there is football hooliganism. Having been previously stationed at Leeds I know that for a fact; and I know all about the cancer in our society that football hooliganism has become."

"With respect sir, what few supporters the Town still have are nothing like Leeds United supporters."

Screwer glared at him. If Hawks had been the office door the paint would have blistered. "Respect?" he screamed. "Respect, Sergeant Hawks? You aren't showing me any frigging respect! If you were you wouldn't be arguing with me, you would be making plans to adequately police Frogley Town's opening game of the season!"

Hawks bit his lip. Retirement and that cottage in the Lakes suddenly seemed much farther away. "Yes sir."

Screwer drew in his horns a little. "Football supporters are the same the world over, Sergeant. Animals. Nothing more, nothing less. Take my word for it, just because the fans of Frogley Town have yet to reveal their true colours doesn't mean to say that one day they aren't going to."

"No sir."

The horns shot back out again as if spring-loaded. "Well just let them! They will not find the Frogley Police Force wanting. Not while my name is Herman Screwer they won't. We'll be ready for them, Sergeant. Ready to whip then into line; ready to break them; ready to smash the brainless bastards into submission!" He suddenly smashed his right fist into his left hand. The splat of the bone of his knuckles colliding with the flesh of his palm made Hawks wince. "Crowd control, that's the name of the game. What are we like for tear gas?"

AIR MAIL

14 Longfields St
New Mills
STOCKPORT
Cheshire
SK 31 8BD
19th March 2006

Air UK Ltd
Stansted House
Stansted Airport
Essex
CM24 1QT

Dear Air UK

I recently travelled with your airline, and what an exciting experience it was! It was the very first time that I have ever flown, but you can rest assured I will be flying with Air UK on many more occasions in the future if my first experience was anything to go by. Everything about the flight was excellent - although I believe Air 2000 could give you a run for your money as far as the in-flight catering goes with their truly mouth-watering lasagne - but what excited me the most was the sight of your stewardesses. How lovely they looked in their smart Air UK uniforms! And this gets me to the point of my letter. Is it possible to buy an Air UK stewardess uniform? I'm sure that if my wife owned one and she wore it at the appropriate time it would be all that was needed to but a bit of spice back into our sex life.

I look forward eagerly to your reply.

Yours sincerely

T Ravenscroft (Mr)

Air UK's reply follows

DEAR CUSTOMER SERVICES

14 Longfields St
New Mills
STOCKPORT
Cheshire
SK 31 8BD

29th May 2007

The Jacob's Bakery Ltd
P.O.Box 1
Long Lane
Liverpool
L9 7BQ

Dear Jacob's Bakery

I am writing to you in my official capacity as secretary of the New Mills Invalids Club. This year marks the 25th anniversary of the club, and we mean to celebrate the occasion in some style, whilst at the same time giving club funds a much needed boost. To achieve this we intend to manufacture and sell to the general public a chocolate biscuit. We are confident that we have the expertise to accomplish this as four of our members used to work for the local sweet and confectionery factory - in fact it was because they worked at the local sweet and confectionery factory that they became invalids, having caught various parts of their anatomy in the machinery, but that's another story.

Here is where you come in. I have long been a fan of your Jacob's Club biscuits, as have many of my fellow members, and to this end we would like to 'cash in' on your esteemed name by calling our biscuit a 'Jacob's Club Foot' biscuit. This would at once inform the public that it is a quality product, and also that it supports invalids. Can I have you permission, please?

Yours faithfully
T Ravenscroft (Mr)

Jacob's reply follows.